Angus Adams:
the adventures of a free-range kid

Lee. M. Winter

© Lee. M. Winter 2015

ISBN-13: 978-1517079246

ISBN-10: 1517079241

For Dane and Lochie

Chapter 1...1

Chapter 2 7

Chapter 3 14

Chapter 4 22

Chapter 5 27

Chapter 6 33

Chapter 7 40

Chapter 8 50

Chapter 9 52

Chapter 10 61

Chapter 11..66

Chapter 12 75

Chapter 13 78

Chapter 14 83

Chapter 15 92

Chapter 16 98

Chapter 17..104

Chapter 18 117

Chapter 19 124

Chapter 20..128

Chapter 21 133

Chapter 22 136

Chapter 23..142

Chapter 1

The Vomit and the Phone

Angus Adams was starting to feel a little uneasy. Things were not going well in the classroom of 5/6A. The immediate problem was that Ryan Evans was going to vomit. Beneath the fiery red hair, his face was the colour of sour cream, he was clutching his stomach and, most persuasive, he was *saying* he was going to vomit.

Unfortunately, Miss Kirkland seemed less convinced. She was in a 'mood' this afternoon and when Miss Kirkland was in a mood you did what she said, when she said, if not sooner. You didn't talk and you certainly didn't ask questions. You kept your head down and your bum up and avoided eye contact at all cost. Eye contact with a moody Miss Kirkland was the equivalent of a World War I soldier at Gallipoli sticking his head up out

1

of the trench to have a bit of a look around. You were likely to get it blown off. Or, at least, yelled off.

"Do you think I'm stupid?" she asked poor Ryan who was cowering before her. "Seriously, do I look stupid?"

Two different questions, thought Angus, but he knew better than to point it out.

"I've lost count of the number of times you've claimed to be feeling sick lately, Ryan," Miss Kirkland continued, "but it's always just before maths. I wonder if anyone else can see a pattern."

Of course, Perry Pritchard immediately stuck up his hand only to have it snapped at him that the question had been rhetorical. Angus watched Perry scratch 'rhetorical' into his little leather pocket notebook of new words (at first break he'd told him he was in a *quandary* over whether to eat his strawberries first or his Tiny Teddies). Finn muttered that Perry was a dork. Angus agreed.

Looking like an angry butterfly in her floppy flowery top, Miss Kirkland sighed and told Ryan to sit down.

"And now you, Luke," she said, moving on to the next problem.

Luke was what Angus's mother would call a 'difficult' child. To be fair, he was a perfectly nice, friendly, well-behaved boy ninety percent of the time. But for the other ten percent he was not nice or friendly and certainly not well-behaved. There was no denying he suffered from anger management issues and no secret he hated maths, which is why he was currently refusing to move to his desk and take out his maths book.

"Luke, let me make it clear that I am *not* putting up with this today. Leave the computer and move to your desk. Now."

Luke ignored her completely as though deaf. Angus knew things were about to get interesting. Normally he might find this mildly entertaining but he was too busy watching Ryan, next to him, whose sour cream face was now distinctly tinted with shades of avocado, which is only a good combination if you're talking nachos.

"You okay?" Angus whispered. Little beads of glistening sweat had popped out all over Ryan's forehead like morning dew on lawn but Ryan just looked back at him with big wet eyes. He clearly wasn't faking it. Angus knew he should do something. But *what*? Any speaking up on Ryan's behalf was going to mean eye contact with Miss Kirkland. This was going to take some serious guts. Did he have serious guts?

To make matters worse, the classroom phone kept ringing as though it was unaware that now was *not* a good time. As its shrill chirp carved the air, Layla – this week's class 'receptionist' – bounced over to answer it, all dimples and swinging ponytail. She called out in her sing-songy voice that it was Hamish's mother *again* asking to speak to Hamish. Up the front, Miss Kirkland rubbed her temples.

Hamish was Angus's closest friend. Kind of his best friend except that best friends were more of a girl thing. They had best friends or best friends forever (BFF), second best friends and often third best friends. It was a mystery how they kept track of it. Of course, Layla probably had it all noted somewhere on her mobile phone (*her* mother wouldn't need to call the class phone). It was a bit stupid, wasn't it, for kids in Grade 5 to have their own phones? And Angus wasn't even a bit envious. Well, not really.

The beads of sweat were now having relay races down Ryan's face. Angus dug deep and summoned up all the guts he could find.

"Ah, excuse me, Miss Kirkland, but I really think that Ry–"

"Not, now Angus," said Miss Kirkland without moving her gaze from Luke, who was still refusing to budge. The class had gone quiet. All eyes moved between the teacher and Luke as though it was an exciting tennis match.

In an icy tone (way scarier than when she yelled) Miss Kirkland informed Luke he had one last chance to move to his desk before there were *consequences*. Luke, finally looking up, and using his own icy tone, told her what she could do with her consequences. Look out, thought Angus, Miss Kirkland's going to lose it.

Miss Kirkland lost it.

"LUKE! GO TO YOUR DESK, NOW!" she screamed. And then everything happened at once. The phone rang again. Layla jumped up to answer it at the same time that Luke finally left the computer. But he didn't move towards his desk. Instead, he made directly for the door.

"Hamish, it's your mother again," sang Layla.

"Oh no, you don't!" shouted Miss Kirkland making a lunge for Luke who was halfway across the room.

"Run out of this classroom and you'll be headed for a visit with the Principal, young man," she said as she managed a grip on his shirt collar.

Next to Angus, Ryan started to make weird throaty noises.

"Miss Kirkland," tried Angus again in desperation, "I really think—"

"Angus, interrupt me once more and you can go with him!"

"Miss Kirkland," called out Hamish, holding the phone, "my nana's knitting me a beanie and Mum wants to know if you could please measure my head?"

"OH MY GOD!" screamed Layla, jumping up from her desk, eyes locked on her pulled-out tidy tray. "My phone's gone! Someone's stolen my phone!"

Luke ripped himself free from Miss Kirkland's grasp and escaped out the door as Angus pushed back his chair and made a frantic dash towards the sink to grab an empty ice-cream container for Ryan. He'd just put his hand on one when he heard a wet, retching sound from behind him as though someone had upended a bucket of wet cement. He turned around. Ryan had vomited all over his desk. Thick wet chunks dripped onto the carpet.

Miss Kirkland stood in the middle of the room looking stunned. Could things get any worse?

Of course they could.

Chapter 2

A Very Good Thing and a Very Bad Thing

A loud fart echoed around the hall from somewhere up the back. Angus bit down on his lip, trying not to laugh while next to him Hamish's body was silently shaking. The whole school was gathered for afternoon assembly. Other kids snickered, guffawed or snorted in less successful attempts at self-control.

Up the front, Mr Dingwall, the Principal, announced he was not amused and demanded to know who the culprit of the offending fart was (no one came forward) and did everyone else think it was funny, did they? Of course they did but even Perry kept his hand down.

With the crowd under control again, Mr Dingwall returned to his rant over the recent thefts of smart devices. The school had implemented a new policy called Bring Your Own Device and if you were lucky enough to own an iPad, tablet or laptop you were allowed, *encouraged* in fact, to bring it to school for use in class. Unsurprisingly, in Angus's opinion, a person or persons

7

were now helping themselves to other people's devices willy-nilly. Specifically, one laptop, two iPads and one tablet had gone missing and with the addition of Layla's phone today, it was apparent the thief was now branching out into mobile communications.

While Angus didn't have his own phone, he had just received a much longed-for iPad for his tenth birthday. But he had no plans to bring it to school. At least once a term he lost his hat, lunch box or pencil case and was under no illusions about his ability to hang on to something as expensive as an iPad. And this was just as well because his mother had said it would go to school over her dead body which Angus thought was a little extreme, but that was mothers for you.

Like a couple of angry caterpillars going head-to-head, Mr Dingwall's eyebrows jumped fitfully as he reiterated that this sort of behaviour WILL NOT BE TOLERATED and the thief or thieves WILL BE CAUGHT. For emphasis, he stabbed a stubby finger at the air with each word.

Angus shifted his behind uncomfortably on the hard floor and silently wished the Principal would hurry up and move on to what he hoped was coming next.

And finally he did. Dingwall rearranged his face into what passed for a smile, but only just.

"And now," he said, "onto a more pleasant item. As you all know, our Robotics club have been working hard recently in the lead up to the regional Robotics Championship, which many of you watched last week here in our very own hall." Angus sneaked a nervous grin at Hamish.

"It gives me great pleasure to announce that the winning team, with their champion robot, the..uh...Death-o-nator...is- "

Angus's heart gave its own drum roll.

"Angus Adams and Hamish McLeod!"

There it was. Through a sea of high-fives and back pats, they made their way up to the front of the hall. With his heart still thumping, Angus had to admit this was pretty cool. They always tell you that winning isn't everything but, jeez, it's not nothing either. And he and Hamish deserved it. Their Death-o-nator robot, designed and built by the two of them, had smashed the opposition from five other schools out of the ring, literally. On the day, it looked as if the title was theirs but then the team they'd beaten in the final round had lodged a protest – something about their robot breaking a technical rule – so they'd had to wait a whole agonising week to hear the final decision.

"The protest was dismissed by all three adjudicators, boys. Well done," said Mr Dingwall as he pumped Angus's hand with a meaty paw. Mrs Nesbit, their Robotics instructor, clapped wildly from the sideline, pausing to give him a thumbs up when she caught Angus's eye. Mrs Nesbit looked like your garden variety grandmother, think pink cardigans and grey bun. You expected her to know more about knitting than robotics. But you had to give the woman her due. She knew her EV3s from her RSXs and what she didn't know about psyching out the opposition wasn't worth knowing. At the regionals, her advice to Angus and Hamish had been to send the competition home crying, in a fair and sportsman like way, of course.

Handing the boys each a laminated certificate, Mr Dingwall said, "And, of course, as winners of the regional competition you will both be going to Sydney next month to compete in the national championships."

The hall again broke out in applause. Mrs Nesbit actually punched the air. Angus and Hamish grinned again at one another in surprise. No one had said anything about *this*. Going to Sydney for the Nationals. *Them*. That wasn't just cool, that was totally awesome.

Back in their places, the boys risked whispering to each other as Dingwall droned on about playground litter. Hamish was concerned his overprotective mother wouldn't let him go to Sydney all by himself. Angus pointed out he wouldn't actually be by himself and surely they'd each be allowed to bring a parent with them. Still, Hamish said he wasn't sure he even *wanted* The Helicopter to come. He called his mother 'The Helicopter' (not to her face, of course) due to her tendency to hover over him at all times in her firm belief this was necessary to keep him safe from asthma attacks, accidents, stray dogs, 'bad' people and insect bites. Angus thought Hamish was a bit unfair to his mother who was a nice lady, never missing an opportunity to offer Angus homemade cakes, muffins and assorted pastries as she believed him to be a little on the thin side. She was a bit like a rescue helicopter dropping packages of baked goods.

At home later, Angus leant his bike against the garage wall. A tidal wave of rock music from the 1970s rolled out of the house and washed over him. This meant Dad was home and Mum was not.

In the kitchen his Dad was cooking spaghetti bolognaise. He turned the music down a couple of notches and tossed Angus an onion.

"There you go, mate. Just in time."

As Angus chopped (with swimming goggles on for onion fume protection) he filled his dad in on winning the robotics regionals and the trip to Sydney. Liam, Angus's younger and only brother, looked up from his homework at the kitchen table and stopped picking his nose long enough to comment on how unfair it was that he wouldn't be able to go to Sydney. Then he went back to his homework with one hand while the other continued trying to remove a stubborn booga that was putting up a fight.

Angus pushed the onion and mince around the pan with a wooden spoon. It was now sizzling and spitting merrily and the kitchen filled with a delicious aroma. Angus opened a can of crushed tomatoes, feeling happy and hungry. There was the slight problem of who he would ask to go to Sydney with him, Mum or Dad, but there was no need to stress about that yet. Just as he was about to pour the tomatoes into the pan, his mother walked through the door. And stopped. She stood there looking at him. This was a bit weird as usually the first thing she did was throw her bag onto the nearest chair and kick off her shoes.

"Mum? What's wrong?" he said, taking off his goggles.

"The school's just called me," she said with an oddly unreadable face. "They want you in the Principal's office immediately."

"Huh? Why? Is this about Sydney?"

"Sydney? What? No, Angus," (of course his mother didn't even know about Sydney yet). "It's about phones. They say you've been stealing them."

Chapter 3

The Very Bad Thing Gets Worse

Twenty minutes later, Angus stood with his mum in front of Mr Dingwall's desk. His knees were wobbly and he felt like he'd been force-fed a loaf of mouldy bread. This was crazy. He hadn't stolen anything. What the heck was going on?

"What do you have to say for yourself?" asked the Principal. With thin lips pinched tightly together in disapproval, he threw a piece of paper onto the desk. Angus and his mother peered at it. A photograph. It showed Angus's tidy tray pulled out and placed on top of his desk. There it was. Up the back left, on top of his Science book and just right of his glue stick sat Layla's sparkling diamante and cat-sticker encased mobile phone.

From somewhere a clock ticked smugly.

Was this a joke? A bad dream?

"Well, what do you have to say for yourself?" repeated the Principal, not laughing and very much

14

awake. Angus opened and closed his mouth and then opened and closed it again. He desperately wanted to speak but his brain and tongue, usually a pretty good team, no longer seemed to work.

Instead his mother spoke. "Angus, is that your tidy tray?"

Finally, his brain found first gear. "Y-yes," he spluttered, "but I didn't put Layla's phone in it. I didn't take her phone!"

Mr Dingwall was unconvinced. He demanded to hear Angus's explanation for how a search of his classroom had resulted in finding the missing phone among his belongings if he himself hadn't put it there. Angus felt heat rise up from his guts. This was ridiculous. He said he had absolutely no idea how the phone had ended up in his tray, repeated he *had not* put it there, and for good measure added that he wouldn't be caught dead with that stupid, sparkling thing if you paid him. This didn't improve things. Dingwall placed his hands behind his back, rocked on his heels and said that now would be a good time to start telling the truth.

"I *am* telling the truth!" Angus felt salt water prick his eyes. He would not cry, he would not cry, he *would not* cry.

"Mr Dingwall," said Angus's mother, "I'll be the first to tell you that my son, like all children, is not perfect. Sometimes he's argumentative, occasionally forgetful and, heaven knows, he can be infuriatingly stubborn. But one thing he is *not*, Mr Dingwall, is a liar. If Angus says he didn't steal this girl's phone then I believe him."

Good old Mum.

"Do you have any other evidence that implicates Angus?"

Dingwall cleared his throat and fiddled with his watch band.

"Er, well, no, not at this stage," he said. "But with respect, Mrs Adams, it *is* fairly strong evidence. I mean to say, we will continue our investigation into this, however—"

"Why don't you have it fingerprinted?" asked his mother with a sigh. "Then you'll know if he's been anywhere near it."

Angus's heart sank like the Titanic. He had no choice but to explain that he had in fact touched the phone that day. At first break, Layla had been passing it around to show everyone a video of a hula-hooping cat. Mr Dingwall said that was very convenient, then wasn't it? Angus said that since he was innocent he in fact found it extremely *in*convenient.

Briskly, Dingwall told Mrs Adams he would appreciate it very much if she would be good enough to please conduct a thorough search of Angus's room at home since several other items of a similar nature had disappeared recently and he was sure Mr and Mrs Adams would prefer to do this themselves than have the police involved.

This was horrifying.

"Of course, this is all very disappointing, Angus," Dingwall continued. "As I said, we will be continuing our investigation, but in the current circumstances it would not be appropriate for you to represent the school at the National Robotics Championships in Sydney next month. I'm sure you understand."

Angus did *not* understand. "You...you can't do that," he said hotly.

But Mr Dingwall said indeed he could and would.

Back at home, Angus's parents searched his bedroom while he looked on from the doorway, his cheeks red hot spots of humiliation. His mother told him she was sorry as she looked in his top drawer under his undies and socks. His dad was poking about in his wardrobe, checking under his old Lego sets, soccer boots, and skateboard.

"Don't worry, mate. It'll be okay," he said closing the wardrobe door. How? wondered Angus. As if reading his mind Dad said he was sure the real thief would soon be caught and then Angus would be cleared and off to Sydney with Hamish. No problems. Absolutely nothing to worry about.

But what if the thief *wasn't* caught? That would be a problem, wouldn't it? And definitely something to worry about.

After searching everywhere there was to search, his parents put on faces that were too cheerful and in a voice that was too bright Mum suggested they should all go and eat dinner. Shaking his head, Angus told her he wasn't hungry and, for once, she didn't insist.

"World's going crazy," said his father on the way out, "You know John from two doors up had his ute stolen the other night?"

After his parents had gone, Angus sat on his Darth Vader doona and stared at his feet. This wasn't a dream. It was a nightmare. In front of the whole school he'd been told he was going to Sydney only for it to be ripped away from him. Worse - everyone at school was going to think he was a thief.

A fat tear rolled down his cheek. Alone now, he didn't try to stop it. It was soon chased by another.

The sound of small feet softly padding into the room made him look up. It was Liam. He put his arms around Angus.

"I'll save you some spaghetti," he said.

Angus tossed and turned and fought with his sheet all night. The sheet won. At 6am he climbed out of bed unsure if he'd slept at all. He dressed quickly. A family of kookaburras shared a joke outside as he pulled on his cross-trainers.

He went down the stairs quietly, hoping to avoid Mum. No such luck. The woman had supersonic hearing.

"That you, Angus? If you're going for a run hang on a sec, I'll come, too," she called.

Pretending he hadn't heard, he was out the door and off before she could say anything else.

The cool morning air was in stark contrast to the burning anger inside him which he took out on the footpath by pounding it as hard as he could. He ran and he ran and was soon covered in a fine sheen of sweat. It felt good to do something so familiar. Especially since everything had become so weird. Once he got into a rhythm, Angus felt he could run forever. Maybe he would.

As he ran he went over the previous day's events for the millionth time. The initial shock had worn off, like a fog lifting, and he was able to think more clearly. *Someone* had put Layla's phone in his tray. That much he knew. But *why*? Was this *someone* out to get him in trouble? Or had his tray been picked at random because *someone* had needed to hide the phone quickly or something?

There was another thing he knew for sure. He wasn't going to take this lying down. There was only one thing to do. He was going to find out who the real thief was, clear his own name and go to Sydney with Hamish. Simple.

Okay, not simple.

Difficult.

Impossible?

Maybe.

But not a thing to lose by trying.

On his way home he ran past the park near the shops and glanced over to see a dark-haired girl kicking a soccer ball. She was alone. He normally wouldn't have noticed, particularly being so preoccupied, but it was an odd sight for this time of the morning. Still too early for the mother and toddler brigade, so the park would normally be empty. Early riser, he thought, and vaguely recognised her as a newish girl in one of the other Year 5 classes. She booted a great left footer and glanced up at him as he went past and, like a punch to the stomach, Angus was acutely reminded that everyone at school would soon think him a thief. Probably today. Wonderful.

Bzzzzzzz! Bzzzzzz! His iPad vibrated impatiently as he pulled off his stinky socks. It was Hamish, Skyping. Figuring it was better to tell him now before someone else did, Angus answered the call and poured out his tale of woe to an open-mouthed and goggle-eyed Hamish who didn't seem to be able to say anything other than "crikey!" As a huge fan of Steve Irwin, the Crocodile Hunter (even though he was, like, dead and everything), Hamish's favourite exclamation was 'crikey' which often got a bit annoying, but on this occasion Angus let it pass thinking the situation did in fact warrant several crikeys.

Once he was crikeyed out, Hamish, being a true friend, didn't hesitate to join Angus in mutual outrage that someone had done this to him and vowed that together they would uncover the truth and *together* they would definitely be going to Sydney or he, Hamish, wouldn't be going either. As his dad would say, he was a good mate. If he'd been a girl, Angus would have declared him the ultimate BFF.

Chapter 4

Nasty Rumours & Awkward Moments

The curious looks, double takes, and downright hostile glares greeted Angus even before he'd finished locking his bike to the rack. Just as he'd thought, rumours of him being the thief had spread through the school like a nasty infestation of head lice.

He told himself he couldn't care less what everyone else thought, held his chin up high and kept his eyes locked straight ahead on the walk to class as people either moved silently out of his way or whispered behind their hands.

He saw Layla as he went up the class steps.

"Layla, it wasn't me. I didn't take your phone," he tried to explain.

She stopped and turned to face him. "Please never speak to me again or come near me or my things," she said and continued on up the stairs with her nose high in the air.

Well, that went well, he thought.

23

Thank goodness for real friends. At first break, the boys all rallied around assuring him they didn't believe for a second that Angus had stolen Layla's phone (there *had* to be another explanation for how it got into his tidy tray) or any of the other missing items. Perry said it was obviously a *stupendous* mistake and Luke offered to beat up anyone who gave Angus a hard time, which was nice of him.

Finn questioned Mr Dingwall's logic in assuming the thief was a student, pointing out teachers, parent helpers and cleaners all had access to the classrooms and adults could be just as devious and underhanded as kids, probably more so, in fact. There was silence as everyone chewed this over along with their sandwiches.

Mr Jackson, the new groundsman, strode past pushing a wheelbarrow of compost.

"Could be him," said Finn. There was silence as this was considered. They all watched Mr Jackson's broad back disappear down the path with the barrow.

"He looks shifty," agreed Hamish as though this were all the evidence required.

Mr Jackson had started at the school after old Mr Barry retired last year. There were unconfirmed rumours he was an ex-soldier returned from armed service in Iraq and was therefore viewed by the kids with a mix of awe and fear. Maybe he'd *killed* people. He was a quiet, serious-looking young man who didn't chit-chat or joke around the way Mr Barry had.

"Yeah, shifty-looking all right," repeated Hamish.

With no further insights from anyone as to who the real thief might be, talk turned to the upcoming Ekka. That is, who was going, who wasn't, how many dagwood dogs Perry had managed to consume last year and the like. Finn said he was going but had a problem as his mother had budgeted for only eight things and he had to decide if he was going to have eight rides in side-show alley, or four rides and four show bags or some other combination. Life was tough.

"What about you, Ryan? You going to the Ekka?" asked Angus in an attempt to pretend everything was just fine and dandy and sure, he could still chew the fat with the guys despite the fact his life was probably ruined.

Ryan, who'd been quiet so far, probably still recovering from yesterday's vomiting incident, looked up and then quickly down again at his lunchbox.

"A-ah, no. Don't think so. With, you know, Dad being sick n' that, we can't really afford it," he said more to his sandwich than to Angus.

An awkward silence followed. Angus mentally kicked himself. If he'd bothered to think for a second about someone other than himself, he would have realised Ryan probably wouldn't be going. His dad had been off work for a few months now with some sort of serious illness and he knew the family were trying to save money for a trip to America for special treatment. Ryan's mum, Mrs Evans, who was also a teacher aide at the school, had been talking to Miss Kirkland about it that morning in a private conversation overheard by everyone.

"I'm not going either," Angus said, clumsily trying to fix things. "We only go every second year and since we, you know, like, went last year, we're not, you know, going...this year." Oh God.

It was the morning for awkward moments as who should now walk by but Layla with her second best friend, Katie-Lyn. Layla turned her face away from the boys as she passed but Katie-Lyn did not.

"Managed to keep your hands off other people's property today, Angus?" she sang over her shoulder.

Angus's stomach tightened and his face heated.

"Leave him alone. He didn't do it," Hamish called after them.

Katie-Lyn stopped and turned around. "I'd watch that new beanie carefully if I were you, Hamish," she said. "Has your nana finished it yet?"

They walked on in a cloud of giggles.

Finn, Perry and Ryan also thought this last comment was pretty funny.

"What?" said Hamish.

Chapter 5

Dragons and a Suspect

All in all, it was a terrible day with everyone pointing, sneering, and whispering and Angus had achieved nothing in the way of finding the real thief. The only good thing was that it was Tuesday. On Tuesdays, he went to Hamish's house after school to hang out. This wasn't possible on other week days as Mrs McLeod filled Hamish's afternoons with one scheduled, structured, supervised activity after another in the firm belief that schedules, structure, and supervision were essential for the healthy development of children. Angus knew this to be her belief because she told him so often. She was undoubtedly a little suspicious of his own parents' more relaxed approach to parenting.

Of course, she also said, children need *some* time for free play so she had scheduled this in on Tuesdays from three-thirty to five o'clock.

He and Hamish fiddled around with the programming of their robot for a while but he just wasn't able to feel any enthusiasm for the task. It was hard not to feel as though robotics had been completely spoiled. And this made him angry. He loved robotics. It was cool to dream up a design and then see if you could make it happen. And of course, at first you couldn't. So you had to think about it. Work out a solution. Problem-solve and then try again until eventually you'd done it. You'd actually created something that could *do* stuff, that you controlled. But with this cloud over his head, with it now being extremely unlikely he'd get to go to the Nationals, he felt it was all pointless.

So he lay on Hamish's bed and watched Frodo the water dragon crawl across his belly. He was, as Hamish said, a little beauty. Hamish had a cool terrarium, home to two young water dragons, Frodo and Bilbo. Hamish dusted a cricket with calcium powder and dropped it into the terrarium for Bilbo's dinner. Frodo seemed more interested in the chocolate muffin Angus held, baked by Mrs McLeod for afternoon tea. Angus lifted him carefully back into the terrarium and munched his muffin.

"We need a plan," he said between bites. "Or at least a starting point if we're going to find the thief. What do we know so far?"

Actually, they knew quite a lot. Refilling the dragons' water from a jug, Hamish repeated what he'd been told by his mother, who was friends with Ryan's mum, the teacher aide.

The known facts were: two iPads had gone missing from classrooms during lunch time, a teacher's laptop had been taken from her desk after school while she was at a meeting, and an Android tablet had disappeared from a lunch bench when one of the senior students had put it down and then accidently left if there, returning in a hurry five minutes later to find it was gone. And of course, they knew about Layla's phone which was no longer missing after turning up mysteriously in Angus's tidy tray.

They agreed that just like in the movies, the thief had to be someone with both motive and opportunity. The thefts had occurred after school and at lunch times. Despite what Mr Dingwall said, Angus felt the culprit was unlikely to be a student as none had access to classrooms after school. Parents could also be ruled out as they generally weren't lurking about the school at lunch times and even the parent helpers usually went home before first break.

Cleaners, who worked before and after school, had to be eliminated for the same reason – no opportunity to commit the lunch time crimes. So that pretty much left teachers, office staff and the groundsman.

Hamish wrote all their thoughts down neatly onto a piece of lined paper headed "School Thefts: Official Suspect List".

Unfortunately, they didn't yet have any actual suspects to write on the list so they sat and stared at each other while waiting for an idea. The dragons chewed their crickets.

"Wanna play Minecraft?" asked Hamish eventually.

Mrs McLeod poked her head into the room. "Have another wee muffin, Angus," she said.

Things were still grim the next morning when they met up again at the bike racks. Neither had come up with any brilliant ideas overnight. Feeling depressed, Angus was about to say the whole thing was hopeless when Hamish elbowed him hard in the ribs.

"Ouch! What–"

"Shhh...look down there!" said Hamish in a half-whisper.

Angus looked. The bike racks were located on the top of a small rise overlooking the staff carpark. There, bending into the boot of his car, was Mr Jackson the groundsman. He was struggling to take out a large cardboard box. The flaps of the box were open and, for a brief moment, Angus and Hamish found themselves staring straight down into its contents – what looked to be a laptop, a couple of iPads, and was that a Nintendo DS?

The boys stared, mouths agape, until Hamish spluttered, "Crikey! Crikey, it *is* him! He's the thief! I told you he's shifty, quick let's follow him!"

Mr Jackson had the box out of the boot and was now headed across the carpark. Hamish took off and Angus scrambled after him.

From a safe distance, they followed Mr Jackson and the box past the office *(the cheek of him waltzing straight past the office!)*, past the Prep classrooms until finally he disappeared around the corner of the school hall, where it was obvious he was headed for his workshop.

The boys peeked cautiously around the corner to see the groundsman struggling to get his key in his workshop door while holding the box under one arm. With a grunt, he managed it at last and disappeared inside. The door shut with a click. The school bell rang.

"Crikey!" said Hamish, still bug-eyed as they made their way back to their classroom. "Crikey!" he said again. He was flushed red in the face all the way up to the roots of his blond hair.

"Stop saying 'crikey'," said Angus.

"Sorry, can't seem to stop. What are we going to *do*? We'll have to go tell Mr Dingwall."

"Calm down," said Angus. "What are we going to tell him exactly? That we saw Mr Jackson with a box of stuff? We only had a quick look inside and there's no way to know if it was the same stuff as what was stolen. I mean, I'm pretty sure I saw a Nintendo DS in there and I don't think anyone is even missing one of those."

"So?" said Hamish. "Someone might have lost one and not realised it was stolen, right? Or maybe we just haven't heard."

"Maybe, but if he stole all that stuff then explain why he was *bringing* the box to school? Shouldn't he be taking it *away* from school? It doesn't make any sense. And why would he put Layla's phone in my tidy tray?"

Hamish considered this. "Yeah, okay. Dunno – it's weird," he admitted.

"We'll talk about it again at first break," said Angus. Despite the speech he'd just given Hamish, he was almost daring to allow himself just the tiniest glimmer of hope that maybe, just maybe, they actually had a suspect now. "But don't say anything to the others – we just don't have enough evidence yet."

Chapter 6

The Girl With the Great Left Kick

The rest of the school day was frustrating to say the least. Angus struggled to concentrate through science and maths and was accused by Miss Kirkland of 'being away with the fairies'. Then at first break, the other boys stuck to him like flies around horse poo and he couldn't get a moment alone with Hamish. Finally, they agreed to Skype after soccer training.

Fortunately, soccer training was cancelled because the coach had broken his toe.

Unfortunately, Hamish's mum saw this as an opportunity for Hamish to do more piano practice rather than risk being unstimulated for five minutes.

At home later, Angus thought he might as well help Dad with dinner. Chicken and veggie pie tonight.

"Uh oh," said Dad peering into the fridge. "We're out of garlic."

"OMG!" shrieked Birdie the budgie over the top of another old music group singing about living in the

34

seventies. (Despite everyone's best efforts, Birdie's vocabulary consisted exclusively of 'OMG' and 'Awesome'.)

"Shoot up to the shop for me, mate?" asked Dad.

The shop wasn't far. About five hundred metres from the end of their street. Angus was the only ten-year-old he knew who was allowed to walk to the shop by himself.

His mum said in *her* day kids were allowed to free-range, which she said meant play in the street, ride their bikes over to each other's houses, climb trees at the park and roll around in the mud if they felt like it. It wasn't called free-range back then. It was just normal.

And apparently nobody died from it. Well, hardly anybody.

Angus *was* allowed to play in the street. The problem was there was no one else in the street to play *with* because all the other kids were at home in their backyards busy with structured, supervised activities. Sure, he had his brother to play with. But still. Someone else would be nice, too.

The park was opposite the shop and, as Angus drew closer, he noticed that same girl once again by herself, kicking a soccer ball into a portable net.

He paid for his garlic bulb, pocketed it and crossed the road to the park and stood for a minute watching her.

Using two soccer balls, she was having a shot at goal with each from about 20 metres out before going to collect the balls. She was good. It was only a small goal and she rarely missed.

"Hi," said Angus when she looked up.

"Hi," said the girl and booted another goal, this time with her left foot. Impressive.

"You're good," he said.

The girl went to retrieve her balls from the goal without comment. Probably already knew she was good.

"I've seen you at school. You new?"

"Yep." She booted two more goals. First the right foot, then the left.

"You play for a club?" he asked.

"Used to. In Sydney," she answered.

At this point, the conversation stalled. Angus had run out of things to ask and she wasn't exactly chatty.

But then as she lined up another kick, she said, "I've seen you at school, too."

Of course. No wonder she didn't want to talk to him. His face got hot.

"I didn't do it," he said before he could stop himself.

The girl looked at him, her own face blank.

Feeling stupid now, he turned and walked away. He was at the footpath when she called out.

"Wanna be goalie?"

He turned around. They looked at each other.

"Okay," he said finally and then remembered the garlic. Pulling it out of his pocket his said, "Just let me run this home. Back in a sec."

She turned away.

When he returned a couple of minutes later, leaping over one of the pine log balustrades that formed the park perimeter, she looked surprised. Didn't she think he'd come back? He went and stood in goal.

Even though the width of the goal area was small, Angus found he had his work cut out for him. The balls came at him hard and fast, high, low and everything in between. And she was accurate. Amazingly so. Especially with her left foot. He'd never seen anything like it.

After about ten minutes they swapped over and Angus had a turn at goal kicking. He wasn't bad but he was nowhere near as good as she was.

They kept on taking turns for maybe half an hour. Later, he realised he'd been having so much fun he'd actually forgotten the terrible trouble he was in. For thirty minutes there'd been nothing but the goal, the soccer balls and the girl.

Then she said she had to go home and the rest of the world came rushing back in. He helped to pack up the goal and realised he didn't even know her name. She must have been thinking the same thing.

"I'm Bodhi," she said, pinning him with that cool stare of hers. "I was named after the tree Buddha sat under to reach enlightenment."

This was the longest sentence she'd uttered so far and for a moment Angus wasn't sure how to respond to the unexpected information.

Then he remembered that any normal person would offer their own name in return. "I'm Angus," he said. "I was named after the lead guitarist in ACDC."

Bodhi nodded. "That's cool."

"Are you Buddhist?" asked Angus.

"No," said Bodhi. "Can you play the guitar?"

"Only on Xbox." They both grinned.

That evening, after a delicious and very garlicky chicken pie, Angus was finally able to Skype Hamish and get down to the serious business of discussing how they might go about investigating Mr Jackson as their chief suspect.

Hamish reported he'd added Mr Jackson to the list as the primary suspect and held it up to the camera so Angus could see it. Angus pointed out he was in fact their *only* suspect. Nevertheless, he agreed that with access to the entire school he certainly ticked the box for 'opportunity'. Motive was more of a problem. *Why* would he be stealing these things?

Neither of them had any idea but further agreed what they needed was to get another look into that box. Angus suggested a recon mission.

"A what?" asked Hamish.

"A recon mission. You know, reconnaissance. Checking things out, getting information. We should at least have a look through the workshop window and see if we can see the stuff or the box."

Hamish thought it unlikely that Mr Jackson would just leave the stuff lying around in full view.

"Got a better idea?" asked Angus.

But Hamish had no ideas, better or otherwise. Angus was about to say goodbye when Hamish's face lit up.

"Hey," he said, "I nearly forgot to tell you that Mum's taking me to the Ekka for my birthday next Saturday and you're invited!"

"Really? Great," said Angus, meaning it. "That'll be awesome. Thanks."

"Ryan's coming, too," said Hamish. "Mum says it'll do him good to have some fun."

"Cool."

It took Angus awhile to go to sleep that night. There was a lot to think about. He and Hamish had discovered Mr Jackson may well be the school thief, he'd made a new friend, well, kind of, who apparently was also allowed to play at the park without adult supervision and now he was getting to go to the Ekka with Hamish and Ryan.

He should be feeling better. But he wasn't. Not really. It was just impossible to feel happy, truly happy, about anything while this stupid stealing business hung over his head.

Eventually he fell asleep and had a weird dream he was at the Ekka with Bodhi kicking chicken pies into a soccer net while Mr Jackson ran away with his show bag.

Chapter 7

Busted!

The plan was to casually stroll past Jackson's room and take a sly glance in at the window while he, Jackson, was safely off working elsewhere on the school grounds. Unfortunately the plan had been immediately thwarted by Mr Jackson himself striding past them into his room just as they got there.

Now Angus stood with Hamish at the edge of the nearby oval, pretending to watch the other kids mucking about. In reality, they were waiting for Mr Jackson to leave his room, hopeful it would happen before the bell rang and they had to abandon the mission.

Time was running out.

"Come ooon!" urged Hamish, nervously hopping from one foot to the other as though desperate to pee. "Hurry up!" Clutching their suspect list in his hand and consulting it again, he said, "Remember, we're looking for two laptops, an iPad and an Android tablet."

Oh no.

Angus had spotted Rapata Takani ambling towards them, flanked by a couple of his dull-eyed cronies.

"Look out," he whispered.

He'd been in Prep class with Rapata who was then, and still was, twice as big as any other kid their age. For some inexplicable reason, Rapata had decided in Prep he was going to hate Angus and pick on him at any opportunity (stomp on his lunchbox, trip him over as he went past, that sort of thing). Angus had long ago given up trying to work out what exactly Rapata had against him in the first place or even trying to make things right between them. Easier just to stay out of his way.

"What are you lookin' at, Adams?" said the mountainous boy, smirking as he neared, his cronies giggling stupidly.

Angus prayed they'd just keep walking and, for a moment, it looked like they would. But then something seemed to occur to Rapata and with an unlikely speed he took a sudden side-step to place his bulk square in front of Angus.

"Hey, you bin pinchin' stuff."

Uncertain if that was a question or statement, Angus remained silent. Rapata was like a dog. He could smell fear in his prey and if he smelt it on you then you might as well start saying your prayers because, like a

Rottweiler with a guinea pig, he was prone to latch his slobbering jaws around your throat and shake you until your brains fell out. So although Angus felt the icy cold fingers of fright clutch at his insides, he didn't look away, flinch or step back.

"Touch *my* stuff and I'll smash yer face in," said the leering mountain.

"Yeah," said one of the cronies.

Rapata bent into Angus's face.

"You got that, Adams?"

He was blasted with oniony breath.

"He didn't do it," blurted Hamish, whom Angus had forgotten was even there.

Just be quiet, thought Angus anxiously.

Unexpectedly, Rapata started laughing. "Good one, McLeod," he said and clapped Hamish on the back, almost sending him reeling before finally skulking off with his buds. His bulky body heaved as he chuckled.

Angus's own body went slack with relief while Hamish groped about in his pocket and pulled out his asthma inhaler.

"He scares the crap out of me," he rasped between puffs.

Their moment of relaxation was short lived. Mr Jackson was coming out of his room. They watched him round the corner in the direction of the office.

"C'mon on," said Angus, just as the bell rang. Ignoring it, they ran up to the workshop amidst all the other kids running helter skelter for class. Pressing their faces urgently to the window, they tried to peer in past the glare. There was a desk and a filing cabinet on the right while on the left was a broad, neatly organised workbench sporting an assortment of tools, more of which hung above from a board stuck to the wall. Near the bench stood a large wheelie bin with a big white label declaring "Lost Property" in fire-engine red letters. It looked to be filled with balls. And a couple of cricket bat handles stuck out.

"I can't see the box, can you?" said Hamish.

"Umm...no...hang on...is that it there - pushed under the bench? See?" said Angus

"Yeah, think it is," said Hamish, following Angus's gaze. Unfortunately the box, sitting large as life under the workbench, was closed.

Angus stepped back from the window.

"Well, this was a waste of time," he said, deflated. "C'mon, we better get to class".

"Look. Door's unlocked," said Hamish who had one hand on the door handle and had pushed it open an inch. In his other hand he was still clutching the suspect list.

"Hamish, no!" said Angus urgently. "We can't just go in. What if he comes back?"

"We'll just take a quick peek in the box and see if any of the stuff has names on it – you know, to identify it as the stolen goods. We won't be in trouble if it means catching the thief." Hamish pushed the door open farther.

"Hamish, I really don't think–"

"I'll just have a peek while you keep a look out," and with that he disappeared through the door.

Jeez. This was typical of him. Charge right in with no thought to the consequences. In Year 2, Hamish had stuck his whole head into a bowl of chocolate cupcake batter the class had made because some idiot had dared him to. Last year, he'd jumped on Mr Barry's idling ride-on mower and ploughed it through a Prep class's geranium bed because "it seemed like a good idea at the time".

Feeling intensely uneasy, Angus peered around the hall corner to keep watch for Mr Jackson. Although he desperately wanted to catch the real thief, he certainly didn't want to end up hauled back in front of Mr

Dingwall's desk in trouble again. Besides, Jackson was ex-army for goodness sake; he could probably kill them both with one hand tied behind his back.

As Angus was thinking this, who should he see but Mr Jackson himself come out of the office and stride purposefully towards the hall. He was coming back!

Angus scrambled to get the two metres back to the workshop door, finding his feet had turned into blocks of cement. He finally got there and thrust his head in.

"Quick, get out of there, he's coming!"

Hamish was under the bench, bent over the now-open box. He straightened up, nearly banging his head, and swung around in fright before losing his balance and knocking into the wheelie bin of balls. The bin went flying and balls bounced into every corner of the room.

Great.

Angus rushed in and frantically scrambled around with Hamish trying to get the balls all back into the bin.

Not fast enough.

"What do you two think you're doing?" boomed a deep voice from the doorway. It was Mr Jackson. He stood glowering down at them. They were busted.

"Who told you to come in here uninvited?"

Hamish's jaw moved up and down wordlessly while his breathing sounded as though he needed his inhaler.

Angus thought fast.

"Ah...um...sorry, um, Mr Jackson. We, ah, lost our ball and, ah, thought someone might have handed it in to you."

Mr Jackson wasn't impressed.

"First of all, the bell rang five minutes ago. You are supposed to be in class. Second of all, you are never, I repeat, NEVER allowed to come in here if I'm not present." A pause. "Do. You. Understand?"

"Yes, Mr Jackson," they both squeaked in unison.

"Now get to class before I report you to Mr Dingwall."

They didn't need to be told twice. They ran back to class, with Angus sweaty-palmed, feeling they'd had a lucky escape. Miss Kirkland screeched at them for being late and put both their names on first reminder.

When the bell rang for home time, Hamish was patting himself down, looking worried.

"I can't find the suspect list," he said to Angus and he pulled out the contents of his pockets: a small rock, ten cents, an unidentified brown lump and a bit of fluff.

"You're kidding me," said Angus as they left the classroom. "You had it down by the oval, what did you do with it after that?"

"I think I might have dropped it in the box," Hamish said quietly. His face had gone the colour of dirty dish water.

"What? What box?" said Angus, impatiently. Then he realised. "You don't mean *The Box*? *Mr Jackson's* box, do you?" Angus now thought of it with capital letters. The Box.

"Shhh!" said Hamish. Ryan and his mother were heading their way. Mrs Evans held a bundle of workbooks.

"Oh, Hamish and Angus. Hi, how are you both?" she said spotting them. Angus groaned inside. Mrs Evans was a bit of a talker and now was not the time for polite chit-chat.

But chat politely he had to. While Angus and Hamish each fidgeted and shifted their weight from foot to foot, Mrs Evans talked of how lovely it was of Hamish to invite Ryan to the Ekka, how excited Ryan was, weren't the two of them excited also, how she hoped the weather would be nice that day and finally about how she really must get on as she still had some work to do in class before she and Ryan could go home for the day. And with that, the two of them finally left the boys alone.

"Oh God, I'm sure I did," groaned Hamish as they approached Angus's bike at the racks. Liam was there waiting patiently to ride home with Angus.

"I left it in the box. I know I did. It was still in my hand and I had to put it down to look at the stuff and then when Jackson came back I panicked, and I think I accidently left it there. And it says on it *he's* our number one suspect!"

"Who's a suspect?" said Liam, "What are you talking about?"

"Nothing," said Angus impatiently. Then to Hamish, "Well, at least it doesn't have *our* names on it. He won't know for sure it belongs to us."

Hamish stared at his feet.

"Oh, no. Please tell me it doesn't have our names on it, Hamish?"

Pause.

"It has our names on it," said Hamish. "I was mucking around with it last night and wrote at the top 'Angus Adams and Hamish McLeod – School Detectives'. It's okay. I mean, we just have to get it out of the box before he finds it."

Angus looked over at the car park to see Mr Jackson struggling to get The Box back into his boot. The Box and the note were clearly going home to his place.

"That might be difficult," said Angus.

Chapter 8

An Opportunity Presents Itself

This was bad. They absolutely had to get that note out of The Box. But how could it be done now that The Box was going home with Mr Jackson? What would he do if he found it?

Worst-case scenario, he might get desperate and try to *silence* them. Well, that was what Hamish had said, very dramatically, but he also admitted that while The Box had contained an assortment of electrical devices, some of the kind stolen and some not, he hadn't been able to see a single item with a name on it. So really, they were still without hard evidence Mr Jackson was even the thief. Still, it wouldn't be good for him to find that note.

There was no further time to discuss it as Hamish's mum was waiting in the car to whisk him away for his maths tutoring.

At home, Dad was helping Liam with his homework at the kitchen table.

"Angus and Hamish are detectives," said Liam.

"Yeah?" said Dad, "What are you detecting? Liam, get your finger out of your nose."

"Trying to find the real thief."

"Good for you. Got any suspects?"

"Not really," said Angus. He wasn't ready yet to talk about Mr Jackson.

"Oh, speaking of school, I've just picked up your new groundsman guy, Bradley Jackson, as a new customer. Gave me a call today after seeing my truck in his street last week. Lives a couple of blocks away. Cyprus St."

You're kidding, thought Angus.

"Paid upfront for a year, combo wash. Seems like a nice guy. No school Monday, for the public holiday, so do you wanna come with me and earn some money? We'll do Jackson's bins, too."

Angus fought to hide his amazement. His dad had given up his career as a chef to run his own bin-cleaning business, which involved much better hours and driving to customers' houses in a cool truck. And now Mr Jackson's house.

Where The Box was.

"Awesome!" said Birdie. Angus couldn't agree more.

Chapter 9

Some Unpleasant Information

So there was some hope. Angus didn't know how he was going to do it but on Monday he was going to have to try to get the note back out of The Box at Mr Jackson's house without getting caught. He didn't dare try it without a good reason for being there on his property and now Dad had given him the perfect excuse. Just had to hope he didn't discover it before then. Tomorrow was Friday and he knew the groundsman didn't work Fridays, so there would be zero chance of The Box coming back to school then.

That afternoon, Angus jogged down to the park on the off chance Bodhi might be there. Frustrated at having to wait until Monday to do anything useful, he needed a distraction. And there she was, doing her thing with the soccer ball.

"Oh, good," she said seeing him. "I need someone to beat."

"Ha, ha." He grinned.

53

As they kicked away, he commented on Bodhi's cool storm trooper t-shirt. Turned out she was just about as big a nut for Star Wars as he was. Had seen all the movies, like a dozen times.

"I've got a Lego Star Wars X-Wing Starfighter to start on at home," he said. It had been a birthday present from Nana. "Wanna help?"

She shrugged. "Sure."

Back at his place he showed her to the phone so she could ring her mum at work and tell her where she was. Then it was down to serious Lego business.

With about five hundred pieces, they soon realised putting the Starfighter together was not going to be a quick job. But they made a start and Angus found Bodhi had a good instinct for the intricate construction required. She had a quiet, self-assured patience he sometimes lacked. As they worked away on it, he started thinking about how Bodhi hadn't mentioned his problems at school. She must know. Surely. All of a sudden, he found he had to know.

"Do you hear kids talking about me? At school," he said casually, not looking at her as he ran his finger down the instruction sheet.

"Sometimes." Bodhi didn't pause in her search through the stack for the piece she was after.

"What do you think?" Angus went out on a limb. "Do you think I did it?" He looked at her now.

"What? Take that girl's phone?"

"Yeah, that."

"No. You didn't take it," she said, still searching through the pile.

"How do you know?"

She shrugged, fixing him now with her level gaze. "Just do."

"Other people think I did," he said glumly.

"Then they're losers," said Bodhi, as if that was that.

After another half an hour of Lego, he was hungry and suggested pancakes.

"You have pancakes?" said Bodhi.

"Well, we'll have to make them."

"Oh." Bodhi admitted she'd never made pancakes before. He assured her it was easy and, before long, he had her whisking and flipping away like a pro.

They made enough for everyone and ate them dripping with vanilla ice-cream and chocolate syrup. Dad and Liam agreed they were the best pancakes they'd ever eaten. Bodhi gave a rare grin, her eyes lighting up as she wiped syrup from her chin.

She was about to leave when Mum arrived home from work.

"Hello, Mrs Adams, how are you?" said Bodhi politely after being introduced. Mum invited her to stay for dinner (not that anyone was very hungry after the pancakes). It was her turn to cook and she was doing a chicken and avocado salad but Bodhi politely declined as her mum was expecting her.

"Nice girl," said Mum after she left.

Mrs Nesbit honked her nose loudly into a tissue that had seen better days.

"Oh, it's just terrible," *honk*, "Who would do this?" *Sniff*.

Angus reached over and pulled another tissue from the box on her desk and offered it to her. She took it, howling loudly.

"I can't afford another one," she said between sobs and honks.

It was Friday morning and, on his way to return the class library box, Angus had been passing the robotics lab when he heard Mrs Nesbit crying. Alarmed, he stuck his head in to check she was okay.

It turned out the thief had wasted no time getting back on the job. Mrs Nesbit had bought a new iPad mini for her little granddaughter who was moving to America. She thought they'd at least be able to Skype each other. It had a lovely Dora the Explorer case and everything, she said, and she'd stupidly left it sitting on her desk from where it had been stolen Wednesday afternoon. She'd thought she was all cried out but, as she was seeing her granddaughter that afternoon, she found herself upset all over again.

Angus was cross. Mrs Nesbit was a great teacher. He tried to imagine Mr Jackson sneaking in and taking the iPad and made a mental note to ask Hamish if he'd seen a Dora the Explorer case in The Box.

He did his best to console her, patting her arm.

"Thanks Angus, love," she said and took her glasses off to dab at her eyes. "Honestly, I wish the powers that be would actually do something about this. But no, all that happens is they point their finger at you, which is the most ridiculous thing I ever heard of, by the way, and just between you and me. I said to them, this is the boy who donated his second-best robot to little Cody Gilbert when his dad ran over his in their driveway, so Cody could still compete at districts. Tell me, I said, does that sound like a boy who steals other people's things? And then, can you believe it, they tell me I've got to find someone else to go to the nationals! Well, I said, there *is* no one else. We won't win if Angus doesn't go, I said." *Honk!*

Mrs Nesbit had defended him. She would. She was one of the good guys. If only he could find her granddaughter's iPad and give it back to her.

Friday afternoon meant swimming training.

Entering the pool with his mother, Angus's senses were assaulted by the chlorine, the cacophony of chattering kids and the barking of urgent instructions from the coaches.

"Toes out, Larissa! Loosen up, Kai!"

They had to crab-walk sideways past the other people to get to the spare seats and await the start of his session. As they passed a snotty-nosed kid from school, the kid snickered and whispered something to his mother. She looked Angus up and down with a face like she'd stepped in dog poo.

He looked away, embarrassed.

Bodhi! He reeled in astonishment. What was she doing here? Well, swimming training, obviously. She was with a lady. Her mum, he guessed. She waved. He waved back and since they were headed that way anyway, he took his mum over. The lady *was* Bodhi's mum. Julie, she insisted they both call her after Bodhi shyly did the introductions.

Like her daughter, Julie was dark and exotic-looking. Her hair was long and loose and one long strand was threaded with beads. She wore a long flowery skirt and a tank top which showed a tattoo of a dolphin on one forearm and a butterfly on the other and she had a tiny gold stud in the side of her nose. She smiled brightly at Angus and he liked her immediately.

In the water, it was soon apparent Bodhi could swim the same way she played soccer – awesomely. Angus, who was also an excellent swimmer, found himself competitively trying to outswim her during the warm-up laps. It was hard going.

He realised to his surprise that it was very important to him that his mum also liked Julie. He tried to keep an eye on them throughout training and was relieved to see them chatting away together. On the way home, Mum said Julie was pleased Bodhi had a made a friend. In fact she'd invited Angus to go down the coast with them on Sunday and Mum said he could if he wanted to. Cool!

That night, however, it became clear not everyone was happy with his new friendship.

"So are you doing everything with her now?" said Hamish on Skype. Was he sulking?

"What?" said Angus, "No, of course not."

"You said *we* were going to make the Lego Starfighter."

Actually, he did feel a bit bad about that. But for goodness sake, couldn't a kid have more than one friend?

"Sorry. But Bodhi was here and you're always busy doing stuff. Anyway, we didn't get it finished."

He really should try to get Hamish and Bodhi to be friends. He and the guys had been playing handball today when Bodhi walked by so he'd called out to her to join in. She played for a while but Hamish hadn't been especially friendly and kept saying Bodhi had hit it out when she hadn't and so the whole thing got awkward, Angus was embarrassed and Bodhi ended up leaving, saying something about having to go to the library.

"It's not my fault I'm busy," said Hamish. Then his voice changed. "You know about the older brother, right?" he said.

"What older brother?"

"Bodhi's."

Oh. Angus had not asked her about brothers or sisters.

"Yeah," continued Hamish, "my mum was talking to Ryan's mum whose sister knows them. They used to live around here a couple of years ago before they moved to Sydney. Mum says the brother's no good. Been to Juvie, you know, like prison for kids. Stealing cars. Mum says they're bad news."

It was like a slap to the face. And was he mistaken or was there a note of glee in Hamish's voice as he delivered this news? He hadn't known Bodhi even *had* a brother but for some reason he felt an overwhelming desire to defend him on Bodhi's behalf. He just wasn't sure how.

"Well, Bodhi's nice and so is her mum." It sounded lame even to *his* ears.

Chapter 10

Blood Everywhere

Angus tossed some lamb shanks, a tin of diced tomatoes and some Moroccan spice into the slow cooker. Since it was Saturday, he had to organise dinner and here it was, sorted at just eight o'clock in the morning.

"You're not bad, you know," said Mum, giving his hair a tousle. "This'll be delicious."

"Want some lessons?" he said.

"Don't push it. Where's your father? You've got a soccer carnival to get to."

Pulling on his shin-pads, socks and soccer boots, he sighed inwardly. Still two whole days until he would have a crack at The Box. Pointless as it was, he wondered if Mr Jackson had found the note yet.

At the soccer field, he joined the team for the warm-up, feeling squeamish in the guts. It was either the fact that things were a bit awkward with Hamish – was it his imagination or was Hamish avoiding eye contact? – or was it the soggy scrambled eggs his mum had made him eat for breakfast? Probably a combination of the two.

To make matters worse, just before the first game got underway, he realised with horror that his shorts were on back to front and the draw string was dangling down his backside. Standing on the sideline, he quickly pulled them off, thinking he could just turn them around and whack them back on again before anyone noticed.

But once he was standing there in his undies he was in such a hurry to get his shorts back on that he accidently put both feet through the same leg hole and fell over. Things went from bad to worse as he tried to get up but found it impossible with both legs jammed tightly together so he lay on the ground flapping about like a demented dolphin while the whole team screamed with laughter, including Hamish.

Eventually Dad came to his rescue and, finally, the first game began. Making a complete fool of himself seemed to have eased some of the tension between him and Hamish. The two of them had been playing together for years, Angus a mid-fielder and Hamish a striker. As the first match began, just like every other match, they easily fell into sync, comfortably anticipating each other's moves.

Five minutes into the game, Angus completed a successful tackle, stealing the ball from the opposition. A quick glance around to see who was clear and he kicked the ball into space on the right of the goal in a well-practised move. At the same time, Hamish feigned his way around his opponent, got to the ball and booted it easily past the goalie and into the net. Score!

High fives all around as all the parents clapped and cheered and called out embarrassing things. Hamish grinned at him. Okay, still friends.

They won the first game 3 – 0 but it went downhill from there as the next two games were lost. He and Hamish were both playing well but it takes an entire team to produce a win and one of their best players was out with the flu. A couple of times he thought about Bodhi and her amazing left kick. Things'd be different if she was on the team. Maybe he could talk her into playing next season. That would go down well with Hamish – *not*.

The day progressed and eventually he ran onto the field for their fourth and final game, looking around for his opposite mid-fielder. He stopped in his tracks.

Dear lord, no.

There stood Rapata, twice as tall and wide as all the other players, meaty hands on hips, smirking at him. He tried to gulp but his mouth was like sandpaper, only drier. Since when did Rapata play soccer?

The whistle blew. At first, things went as he feared they would. Rapata, who wasn't particularly skilled, played like a bully, stomping on his feet with his spiked boots whenever possible and slamming his much larger and heavier body into his at every opportunity. Then it happened.

It was eight minutes into the second half and the scores were dead level at one all. Angus made a successful tackle against one of the more normal-sized opponents and looked for Hamish's feet for a quick pass. But Rapata was having none of it. He came barrelling toward Angus with all the fury of a mad bull, probably hoping to get a good kick in to Angus's shin as well. But large, heavy bodies are hard to stop once they get going with any momentum and so when Rapata's own teammate, who was actually closer to the play but with his back to Rapata, decided he was going to have a crack at a tackle, Rapata was unable to slow down in time, smacked straight into his teammate, knocked him flying and went down in a heap himself, landing awkwardly and twisting his left ankle in the process.

As he went down, his right leg slid out in front of him causing Angus to trip over it and fall hard on top of him with an unfortunate but entirely accidental elbow to the face. The result was that Angus had knocked out one of Rapata's front teeth. There was blood everywhere and the game was stopped for a good five minutes while Rapata was taken off the field, limping, and the blood mopped up. He looked at Angus murderously as he passed.

"I'm gonna get you, Adamth! You're *tho* dead!"

A number of players, on both sides, were looking at Angus with awe and unbridled respect. Others less so.

"Jeez, Adams. You're a piece of work, aren't ya?" It was Flannery, an opposition player and one of Rapata's school cronies. "A thug as well as a thief."

"Like, he can talk," whispered Hamish. "Forget them."

"This is bad," Angus whispered back, "Now I've got to watch out for Mr Jackson *and* Rapata."

He wasn't sure who he was more afraid of.

Chapter 11

A Big Mistake

Examining the sky from his window the next morning, Angus was relieved to see it was clear, blue and cloudless. Perfect beach weather even if the water would still be a little chilly this time of year. He was looking forward to wearing his new elbow-to-knee wetsuit.

Charging down the stairs two at a time, the plan was to scoff some breakfast quickly before Bodhi and her mum came to pick him up at nine. But he stopped in his tracks at the kitchen door. Sitting at the table, Mum and Dad did not look happy.

"What?" he asked.

"I was talking to Hamish's mum at soccer yesterday," began Mum.

With his appetite sliding away, Angus had a bad feeling about where this was heading.

"She told me some things about Bodhi's family that I wasn't aware of."

The best strategy here was to beat her to it. "You mean about her brother?"

"Yes, I mean about her brother. You didn't tell me that Bodhi has an eighteen year old brother," said Mum, frowning.

"I didn't *know* she had a brother until Hamish told me," he tried to explain. "So what, anyway?"

"Apparently the brother's been in trouble with the law."

"What's that got to do with Bodhi?"

"Given that we've just met the family, I'm just not sure now that you should be going to the coast with them today," said Mum.

What? This was totally unfair!

"Why not?" he demanded, "Bodhi can't help what her brother's done. Why should it have anything to do with us?"

"Angus–" started his mother but he cut her off.

"Anyway, you like Bodhi and you like Julie. Dad?" Angus pleaded desperately to his father. "Aren't you two always saying everyone makes mistakes? So Bodhi's brother made a mistake. He's paid for it, right, so he should be allowed another chance!"

"Angus," said Dad, putting down his spoonful of Weet-Bix that had been halfway to his mouth, "this one's your mother's call. There's no rush. You can go to the beach with them another time, after we get to know them all a little better."

"This is so unfair! So what, am I still allowed to play soccer with her at the park?"

"Of course," said his mother, "I don't mind you being her friend. I just don't want you driving miles away with them, just yet."

Angus stomped backed to his room and sat, shoulders slumped, on the edge of his bed. He looked at Darth Vader.

"Now what I am going to do today?" he said out loud. But Darth remained silent. It was so totally unfair he couldn't go to the beach with Bodhi and he really wanted to try out his wetsuit. Well, if he couldn't go with Bodhi, maybe Hamish could talk his mum into taking them both to the beach. He knew his own parents probably would, too, if he asked them, but he felt too angry with them to do so.

So with swimsuit, towel and wetsuit tossed quickly into a backpack, he went to face his parents again. Mum was washing up.

"Is it okay if I ride around to Bodhi's place and tell her I can't come?" he said. "She thinks she's supposed to pick me up."

"Sure," said Mum over her shoulder.

"Then I'm going over to Hamish's. Okay?"

"Okay, but don't forget you promised your father you'd mow the lawn later."

"I'll be back for that."

"Huh…" said Dad, peering at the newspaper. "There was a car stolen from the staff carpark at the school last week. School just can't take a trick at the moment," and he shovelled in another spoonful of Weet-Bix.

It was lucky Bodhi had previously pointed out her house to Angus. He had no trouble navigating his way through the sleepy, Sunday morning streets up the hill to the big old house with the wide verandas. In the driveway was an older model, green Ford station wagon with two surfboards lashed to the roof racks. He wheeled his bike up to the front steps. A set of wind chimes pealed out a greeting.

As he went to put his foot on the bottom step, the screen door banged open and Bodhi bounded out and down the steps.

"Oh, hi," she said when she saw him. "Weren't we picking you up?"

Before he could answer, Julie and an older boy appeared from inside, laden with bags, towels and boogie boards.

"Hi, Angus, love, good timing. We're just packing the car. Have you met Taj?"

"Dude," said Taj. Putting a bag down, he stuck out his hand. He had his mother's broad smile.

"Hi," said Angus, shaking his hand. He looked like your typical surfer dude with wild hair that stuck out everywhere and a cool-looking shark tooth hanging around his neck.

"Jump in, you lot. We're off," said Julie. She chucked all the gear in the back of the station wagon and tried to slam it shut. The catch wouldn't quite click in so Taj helped her by giving it a shove.

"That's got it," she said. "Come on, hop in. Beach is best early in the morning."

The others started piling into the car.

"You coming, Angus?" called Bodhi, moving over on the back seat to make room for him.

"Ah...yeah, sure," he said, not quite believing what he was about to do. "Of course." He jumped in.

Off they went, down the highway towards the sun, surf and sand of the coast, Angus and Bodhi in the back and Taj in the front with Julie.

Angus immediately felt sick with guilt. In the split second he'd had to make the decision, jumping in the car had seemed easier than awkwardly trying to explain he wouldn't be coming, after all. This was the first time he'd ever done anything this seriously bad. More like Hamish to do something this stupid and impulsive. What had he been thinking? If his parents found out, he'd be in big, big, trouble. But what could he do now? There was no way he could ask Julie to turn around.

It was a warm day. With the windows wound right down, the wind whipped against his face.

"You surf, dude?" Taj shouted from the front. It was hard to hear over the wind.

Angus, yelling, explained that no, he didn't really know how to surf but would love to give it a go.

"No probs," said Taj with a grin.

Eventually, the old station wagon left the highway and traversed the local coast streets into Main Beach and the labyrinth of tourist apartment high rises. Julie said she knew a good side street to park in where they wouldn't have too far to walk with all the gear. As they parked, Angus watched a family with two little kids go by, headed towards the ocean, four sets of thongs all *thwack, thwacking* together on the cement in a happy symphony. The little girls were swinging brightly-coloured buckets and spades. One of them smiled at Angus and he smelt coconut sunscreen.

They all piled out of the Ford.

"Angus, grab a boogie board, dude," said Taj, pulling one from the back. Everyone grabbed some gear.

"Let's go." And with that, they were making their own *thwack, thwack*, noises up the path towards the beach.

The surf roared like a mighty beast, the breeze carried the scent of salt spray, and the sand oozed soft and warm between his toes. Impossible not to feel a little better. Here now, so might as well try and enjoy the morning. Face the consequences later.

And a fantastic morning it was. Bodhi was only just learning to surf and happy to share her board with Angus. While still on the sand, Taj showed them how to lie on the board and then jump up to standing. 'Pop-ups' he called them. After about twenty practice pop-ups Angus and Bodhi took the board out into the water to give it a go on a real wave. The surf was perfect for beginners, Taj said, with calm, crumbling waves. From under a purple and yellow beach umbrella, Julie watched Bodhi and Angus take turns at falling off, laughing at each other's lack of skill. After about an hour of this, they gave it up in favour of the boogie boards they were both more competent with and spent another hour between the flags, catching waves in fast and furiously dodging the little kids in the shallow water. Later, on the sand, they watched Taj surf, admiring how he made it look easy and vowing to keep practising themselves.

When it was time to lug everything back to the car, Bodhi and Julie walked ahead with Angus and Taj behind.

"You're not bad for a beginner, dude," said Taj.

"Yes, I am. I spent the whole time falling off."

Taj laughed. "Everyone does at the start."

"Okay."

"Having some trouble at school, that right?"

"Um, yeah." So Taj knew. Great.

"In here," Taj said. Angus looked up. Taj smacked his own chest with his fist. "This is what counts, in here. Believe in yourself. Always hold your head up, dude."

In between two trendy restaurants, all shiny chrome and glass, was wedged a tiny old-fashioned takeaway. At a plastic table out the front, they ate burgers the size of their heads and Angus suffered brain freeze from a chocolate thick-shake so thick it was almost impossible to suck it up through the straw.

On the drive home, he rested his head back on the seat. He was sandy, salty and again, now that home was drawing nearer, sick with guilt. No one spoke much as it was too hard to yell over the wind. Bodhi never talked much anyway. She was definitely a girl of few words who just didn't seem to feel the need to constantly be yabbering on. Hamish, on the other hand, was a constant talker saying whatever popped into his head, *whenever* it popped into his head. Angus's whole family were yabberers also, so the house was always filled with noisy chatter. Bodhi's quietness, her stillness, made a nice change.

Riding his bike back from her place, he considered his situation. Best-case scenario was his parents never found out he'd defied them and gone to the coast with Bodhi. Worst-case scenario was they already knew and he was about to be grounded for the rest of his life. If that happened he wouldn't be able to go with Dad to Mr Jackson's tomorrow.

He didn't have to wait long to find out. Swinging his bike into the driveway, he saw his mother standing at the front door. She did not look happy.

"How was the beach, Angus?" she asked.

Chapter 12

Consequences

"Disappointed doesn't even begin to cover it."

"I know, Mum, I–"

"No. You don't get to talk yet." She and Dad were standing in front of him, while he sat, cringing with shame before them, guilty as charged and awaiting sentencing. A morning phone call from Mrs McLeod to discuss plans for Hamish's birthday had undone him.

"We give you a lot of independence, Angus. You know that. And we've always been proud of it. And proud of the way you handle it. But today..." his mother trailed off, shaking her head.

"We feel let down, mate," said Dad.

"I'm really sorry," Angus tried lamely.

"Not the point," said his mother. "You made a conscious decision to disobey a very clear instruction. Now you'll have to live with the consequences. Honestly, I'd have thought you had enough of being in trouble lately." She exchanged a look with his father. Here it comes, he thought.

"I know you're expecting to be grounded," she began, "but we've decided against that."

Angus shot his head up. "What? Really?"

"Grounding would mean you miss out on work tomorrow with your father, when I actually think it will do you good to work hard for a day," said Mum.

"*Very* hard, in fact," said Dad. "But...you will be donating all of the money you earn to a charity."

Oh. This was a bummer as he had thought of putting the money towards buying his own surfboard. Still, at least he would be able to go with Dad to Mr Jackson's place and look for The Box.

"Grounding also would have meant you couldn't go to the Ekka with Hamish for his birthday. And while I would have happily deprived you of that, I don't think it's fair to ruin Hamish's day," said Mum. "Instead, you will work in the garden every afternoon this week for an hour after school."

Inwardly, he sighed with huge relief. He was getting off pretty lightly, all things considered.

"And," his mother continued, "your iPad is off limits for one week."

Nooooooooo! No iPad for a week! Unbearable!

"Any questions?"

Knowing better than to complain, he shook his head.

"I'm sorry for letting you down," he said instead.

"Good," said Dad. "Now go and mow the lawn."

Chapter 13

The Box

Monday morning and the holiday from school was finally here. Angus pulled the doona up over his head and groaned. Now it was here, he felt sick with dread thinking about going to Mr Jackson's place in the hope of retrieving the note from The Box. Especially after getting into such trouble yesterday.

Somehow he had to not only get access to The Box but find the note Hamish had dropped (which had their names on it *and* Mr Jackson's - identifying him as the prime suspect in the school thefts, no less!) all without getting caught.

"You can do it, Angus, you have to," Hamish had said at school.

Could he do it? Of course he couldn't do it! How on earth was he going to do it?

Usually he enjoyed working with Dad, driving around in the truck high above the traffic. On arrival at a customer's house, he would go and get the bins for Dad who would lift them up into the washing bay on the back of the truck, wash them with the high-pressure hose and lift them down again. After they'd been deodorised and dried, Angus took them up to the customer's house, ticked them off on Dad's run sheet and read out the name of the next customer. But as they came closer and closer to Mr Jackson's name on the run sheet, Angus felt sicker and sicker.

"You all right, mate?" asked Dad looking at him.

"Yeah, I'm okay," said Angus who was definitely *not* okay and had half a mind to tell Dad he felt terribly unwell and could he please go home to Mum immediately? But he couldn't do that. There was no way they could let Mr Jackson find that note. If he *was* the thief then there was no telling what he might do to him and Hamish if he knew they suspected him. Of course, there was no telling what he might do to him if he found him rifling around in The Box but he tried not to think about that. Anyway, surely The Box would be inside his house somewhere, impossible to get to? He kind of hoped it was.

All too quickly, they arrived at Mr Jackson's place. There was no sign of Jackson himself but his green garbage bin and his recycling bin were out on the footpath. Angus chewed his nails nervously and watched the house as Dad washed the waste bin first.

"Okay, mate, he wants them round the back," said Dad, pushing the green waste bin towards him. Dad would now move on to the recycling bin.

This was his opportunity. Now or never. He grabbed hold of the bin and pulled it along the driveway down the side of the little fibro house. Out the back were a veranda and small backyard with a single detached garage sitting at the end of the driveway. Angus knew he had to move fast. No sign of anyone out back and the house looked quiet. Good, probably not home. He left the bin, ran up to the small garage window and peered in. He could see Mr Jackson's car, some tools and boxes, but not *The* Box. Wait! *His car*?? Gosh, did that mean he *was* home?

Looking around wildly, he expected any second to see a furious Mr Jackson come striding out the back door demanding to know why Angus was looking in his garage window. But nobody came out, furious or otherwise, and as he glanced toward the back door he was shocked to see –

The Box.

Sitting on the veranda, unmistakeable and bold as brass. Angus hesitated. He knew Dad would be almost finished with the recycling bin. The Box sat there mocking him.

"Here I am; what are you going to do about it?" it seemed to be saying.

Okay, go! Heart pounding, he leapt up the three steps to the veranda and pulled open the flaps. There was all the stuff - iPads, a laptop, and yes, a Nintendo DS. Angus began to hunt for the note, frantically moving items aside. As he searched, he heard voices from around the front.

"Yeah, lovely day for it," Dad was saying. "My son has taken your green bin round the back. Angus. Maybe you know him from school?"

Panic rose in him like a tidal surge as he realised Mr Jackson was out the front with Dad. Shutting The Box he hurtled down the steps and bolted back around the side of the house. Mr Jackson was standing with Dad. He looked a bit weird in a t-shirt and shorts instead of the usual overalls but he looked up and smiled at Angus. This was weirder still because he *never* smiled.

"Hi, Angus. We kind of met last week, didn't we?" he said, obviously recognising him from the workshop incident.

"Ah...hi," Angus stammered. Then, unbelievably, Mr Jackson stuck out his right hand for him to shake.

"Well, it's good to officially make your acquaintance," he said, his enormous mitt pumping Angus's. "You're a good bloke for helping your dad on a holiday."

Angus tried to swallow a football-sized lump and wondered if anyone else could hear his heart drumming inside his chest.

Chapter 14

Ambushed

"What do you mean, it wasn't there? Of course it was there!" said Hamish. Angus passed him a cricket from the jar. They were feeding the water dragons after Hamish had been awarded some rare free time and Angus had finished work. He'd told his tale of The Box search with Hamish annoyingly interrupting at every opportunity.

"I'm telling you it wasn't there," he said.

"Did you look properly?" demanded Hamish, dropping the cricket into the terrarium. Frodo pounced on it. "I mean, crikey, you said you were rushed, so maybe you missed it."

"I didn't miss it. It just wasn't there. Maybe you lost it on the oval. With luck a cleaner picked it up and just chucked it in the bin thinking it was rubbish."

"Did you at least look for names on the stuff in The Box?" said Hamish.

"No, I didn't have time to do anything except look for your stupid note."

"Hey, the note's not stupid."

Angus sighed.

"We still don't know it was him in the first place," he said. "Mrs Nesbit's mini-iPad definitely wasn't in there."

"So what? He could have stashed that somewhere else," Hamish said stubbornly.

Angus filled the lizards' water bowl from a jug.

"There's got to be more we can do," he said. "A good detective doesn't get fixated on only one suspect. We need to remember it might be someone else."

"Nup, it's him," said Hamish. "I'd bet my Wildlife Warriors membership badge on it."

The next day, back at school, they decided to tail Mr Jackson over lunch one final time to see if it led anywhere. They watched him add compost to the Year 1's vegetable garden, fix a leaky bubbler at the tuckshop and chat pleasantly with Mrs Nesbit who passed by.

"The hide of him! Talking to her after what he did," said Hamish.

When the bell rang to go back to class, they'd gained not a scrap more evidence.

That afternoon, Hamish headed off to his mother's waiting car and an extra-curricular activity of some sort; Angus couldn't keep track of them all. Liam was going with a friend for a play-date so he would be riding home alone. He put his bag on the ground so he could unlock his bike. But then a strange thing happened. Without warning, his bag went flying out from under his hand. What the heck? Someone had kicked it viciously away. He was suddenly in a huge shadow.

Uh-oh.

Rapata Takani.

"Adams," said Rapata, no longer lisping after a visit to the dentist, "did you think you were gonna get away with it?"

Angus looked around quickly to see who was about. Not a single teacher down in the staff car park. Typical. Where are they when you need them?

"Rapata, it was a...an accident," he stammered, "I didn't me—"

"Shut it!" said Rapata as he lifted his right hand and made a fist clearly intended for Angus's face.

Angus did the only sensible thing he could. He turned and ran. Having the advantage of being a good runner, he scaled the small retaining wall near the bike racks and sprinted across a small rock garden towards the school dental van. Beyond that lay the Office – and safety! He glanced back. Rapata was limping after him. Thank goodness for that sprained ankle. He'd have no problem outrunning him to the office.

"Whoa!" Wrong-footed, he lost his balance, tripped over a rock and was sent sprawling.

Rapata was over him before he could scramble up.

"Ha. Ha," said the giant in a slow sneer and kicked Angus hard in the ribs.

Okay, that hurt. Now what? Curl up in a ball? Or is that for a dog attack? Same thing. He did his best to curl up. From under his arm he could see Rapata take aim for another kick, this time to the head. As the enormous boot came at him, Angus rolled fast to the right and kicked hard with his own foot in a sweeping arc. It caught Rapata on his grounded leg, knocking it out from under him. He came down in a heap. Angus started scrambling to get up and away.

"STOP RIGHT THERE!" shouted a man's voice as he got to his feet. "THE TWO OF YOU, DON'T MOVE!"

Angus, startled, looked toward the voice.

It was Mr Jackson, of all people. From the direction of the Hall, he came running towards them. Great, thought Angus, now I'm going to be in trouble again. But when Mr Jackson reached them, he grabbed Rapata by the shirt collar and dragged him up to standing.

"I saw the whole thing. You're off to the Office," he said. "NOW!" Rapata scowled but limped off, shooting Angus a last menacing glare.

"Are you okay, Angus?" Mr Jackson helped him up. "That was a nasty kick you took."

"Um, yeah, I guess," he said getting to his feet. Ouch! Maybe a rib was broken.

"You're bleeding," said Mr Jackson, pointing to Angus's right knee. It was indeed badly grazed and bleeding.

"Come with me. I've got some Band-Aids in the workshop."

Angus had no choice but to go with him, limping himself a bit now.

In Mr Jackson's workshop, he sat in a chair and held a cloth to his bleeding knee while the groundsman called the office to report the incident.

"Rapata's going to see Mr Dingwall," he said after hanging up. "Now let's get you sorted. How're the ribs? Can you push on them?" It hurt, but Angus could push on them without screaming.

"Don't think anything's broken but you'll have a nasty bruise tomorrow."

He rummaged through his desk drawer looking for a Band-Aid.

Angus looked down and realised with astonishment that The Box was on the floor right at his feet. Right there! He suddenly felt very uncomfortable. And it wasn't just because of his ribs. Was Mr Jackson a bad guy? Were bad guys usually this nice? While he considered this, there was a brisk rat-a-tat at the workshop's open door. It was one of the ladies who worked in the office wanting to speak with Mr Jackson.

While the adults talked in the doorway, Mr Jackson with his back to the room, Angus quietly bent down, slid a finger under one flap of the box and lifted it up. Maybe he *had* missed the note. Another quick look couldn't hurt.

"Looking for something?" He snapped his head up. Oh God. He was dead. The lady had gone. Mr Jackson was looking at him. His face was unreadable.

"I...er...no...I," he began as his face heated up.

Then Mr Jackson did the last thing in the world Angus would have expected him to do. He started laughing.

And not an evil mwah, ha, ha laugh, but a 'you crazy kid' laugh. He reached into his pocket and pulled something out.

"Is this what you're looking for?" He handed it to Angus. It was the note. Hamish *had* dropped it in The Box, after all. They looked at each other. He had no idea what to say but at least Mr Jackson was still smiling.

"I'm not the thief," he said.

Angus was rendered mute, his mouth incapable of forming words.

"I read what's on there. You think all those things in my box have been stolen from the school." It was a statement not a question. "Look at my desk, Angus."

He looked. Actually now he really looked he noticed a laptop with the back taken off, wires and circuitry exposed, and there was a phone in the same condition.

"I was an electrical engineer in the army, Angus. In my spare time I try to fix people's old broken phones and computers and stuff. If I can fix them, I give them to the Kids' Hospital. For the kids to use.

People give me these things, I don't steal them." And there on the wall above the desk was a framed certificate of thanks from the Children's Hospital with a photo of a smiling Mr Jackson and some kids.

Angus hoped for an asteroid to hit Earth immediately and save him from this shame. What an idiot he was. Mr Jackson wasn't a thief. He was the opposite of a thief. He was a kind man who gave his time to fix broken stuff for free and help sick children. Huh, some detectives he and Hamish had turned out to be.

"Sorry," he said quietly, looking everywhere except the man's eyes.

"It's okay. And clearly you're not the thief either or you'd hardly be hunting for the real one."

"I just want to clear my name."

"Understandable."

Mr Jackson applied the Band-Aid to his knee.

On the desk, Angus noticed a second photo. Mr Jackson with his arm around a little girl. Five or six years old, maybe.

"Who's she?" he asked, indicating the picture.

"My daughter. She died."

"I'm sorry," he said again, not knowing what else to say.

"She was in hospital for a long time. The staff were good to her."

Neither of them said anything for a time.

"Look," continued Mr Jackson, finally, "I think it's great that you and your friend are trying to find the thief. But you have to be realistic about your chances. And you definitely don't want to be going into any school rooms without permission like you did the other day or you will end up in even more trouble."

"Okay," Angus said, standing up.

"Just a thought," said Mr Jackson, "but if you're serious about finding the culprit, I'd look closer to home."

"Closer to home?" Angus didn't understand.

"The phone was found in your tidy tray, right?"

"Yes, but–" Angus couldn't finish as Mr Jackson's own phone started to chirp.

"I've got to take this," he said looking at the screen. "You should get going. I hope the ribs aren't too sore."

Angus left and went to find his bag, still unsure exactly what Mr Jackson had meant about looking closer to home.

Chapter 15

An Unfortunate New Suspect

Without his iPad to Skype with, Angus had no choice that evening but to do it the old-fashioned way and telephone Hamish to tell him what had happened.

"Crikey," said Hamish after Angus had finished his story. "I was certain it was him. He sure looks the type. Grumpy all the time."

"He's not grumpy," said Angus. He wasn't going to tell anyone, even Hamish, about Mr Jackson's daughter. Just didn't seem right to. He thought about how sad Mr Jackson must be. Anyway, Hamish seemed to be missing the point.

"At least we know not to waste any more time watching him," he said.

"True," admitted Hamish. "Now you can spend all your time watching for Rapata instead. I bet you pooed your pants when he came after you. Scared he'll try again?"

"I *did not* poo my pants. He's been suspended and told not to go near me. School called Mum before."

"And asked her to come in and pick up your dirty undies, I bet," chuckled Hamish.

"Ha, ha. Anyway, we're back at square one."

"Yeah, so what now? Do we give up?"

"No way," said Angus.

But by the following afternoon they were no closer to having a new suspect. Hamish thought looking for someone with motive didn't really help as obviously whoever it was would likely try to sell the items for money, and everyone likes money and generally wants more of it, so that was motive for *everyone*. Angus partially agreed but also felt some people wanted or needed money more than others.

Standing by the road at the edge of the soccer field, with no one else in sight, they realised after about twenty minutes that training must have been cancelled again. Obviously, he and Hamish hadn't received the message. He didn't really mind as his ribs still hurt a bit.

"Let's just walk home," he said. "It's not far."

Hamish looked doubtful. "The Helicopter will freak," he said.

"Neither of us has a phone to ring our parents so do you have a better idea?" said Angus.

"No," said Hamish. "Okay, let's go. I don't like the look of those clouds." A set of dark, ominous-looking thunderheads had formed in the sky to the south, having seemingly come from nowhere. There was a loud rumble of thunder.

Quickly making their way along the path toward home, they kept their heads down while the wind picked up swirling leaves and dust around them, stinging their bare legs. The clouds moved in fast and it was soon quite dark even though it was only four o'clock. The passing motorists had turned their headlights on. Angus felt a heavy drop of water hit his face.

"Uh oh," he said, "I think we're about to get drenched!"

As if on cue, the sky opened up and the rain teemed down in thick sheets. They started to run, hard bullet-like drops belting their faces and making it almost impossible to see. All of a sudden, Angus was aware of a vehicle pulling up to the curb just in front of them.

It was Julie's station wagon. And Bodhi was with her.

"Quick, jump in the back!" Julie yelled over the rain across Bodhi, who'd wound down her window. They scrambled in.

"Nasty storm. Lucky we saw you," Julie said as she pulled away, the windscreen wipers working overtime. "Wait it out at our place, if you like."

Angus glanced across at the shivering Hamish. He looked uncomfortable, and not just because he was cold and wet as a fish. In the front, Bodhi was as unreadable as ever.

Back at the house, Julie made the three of them steaming mugs of hot chocolate with little pink and white marshmallows bobbing about on top. They drank them in the lounge room near the heater. Angus and Hamish were wrapped in towels while their shirts were in the dryer.

Angus looked around. The house was a rainbow of colours. Bean bags, cushions, rugs and chairs of every colour and texture imaginable. Bright prints in even brighter frames covered the walls and shiny glass beads hung in all the doorways. Julie was doing something in the kitchen. Angus could smell cinnamon.

While they waited for their shirts to dry and the rain to stop, they played 'Guitar Hero, Legends of Rock' on Bodhi's Xbox. She had two guitars *and* the drums! On the second track, they were interrupted by a shout from up the hallway.

"Bodhi! Dad's on the phone, wants to talk to you."

Angus recognised the voice as Taj. Bodhi dropped the drumsticks and raced off up the hallway. She'd told Angus about her dad the other day. They'd been climbing trees that lined the local AFL oval. High above the ground, they sat in the broad fork of two leafy branches, hidden from view, watching the traffic in the street. In her quiet, unhurried fashion, Bodhi told him how her parents had separated and Julie had brought her and Taj back to Queensland while her dad had stayed in Sydney.

'Hotel California' blasted from the Xbox while they waited for Bodhi to return. Angus took over on the drums and Hamish played guitar. At the end of the song, the music stopped. In the quiet, they could hear someone outside on the veranda talking.

"I told you not to call me," the voice hissed angrily. It was Taj. He was just outside the lounge room window. He couldn't see them because the curtain was drawn but there was no mistaking it was his voice. Angus realised he probably didn't know they were there. He was obviously talking on a phone.

"I told you I'm not doing it anymore," Taj said.

He must have been walking around as he talked and every time he walked away Angus couldn't hear what he said, but then he would come close to the window again and he could make out more of the words. Angus wasn't entirely comfortable listening in on a private conversation but he wasn't sure what to do about it. Make some noise to let Taj know they were there?

Before he could do anything, Taj said, "...from the school was a mistake. My little sister–"

Hamish looked at Angus with widening eyes.

"—no...not taking any more...I don't want her to...why can't you just find someone else..."

There was a scraping noise as though Taj was moving a chair to sit down. Hamish bounced up and down in a frenzy, pointing wildly at the window while his mouth opened and closed.

"Okay!" Taj said clearly, "if it will get you off my back, but I'm not going to change my mind. The car park at the shops here on the corner of Saville and Hinchcliffe?...I can't until Friday... four o'clock." He said goodbye and they heard him go down the steps.

Hamish was still opening and closing his mouth and weirdly shaking his head. Angus felt sick. Again. It was becoming a permanent state. Julie came in from the kitchen with their now-dry shirts.

"All good," she said holding them out.

If only it was.

Chapter 16

Scarface and the Gorilla

Angus shifted his weight, trying to get more comfortable. A small, sharp rock was sticking into his left knee and he picked it up with his free hand, threw it away and rubbed at the sore spot. In his other hand he held Dad's high definition video camera. It was Friday and he was kneeling behind the industrial bin at the back of the car park attached to the shops, waiting for four o'clock.

He still couldn't make himself believe Bodhi and Taj had anything to do with the thefts. He'd tried in vain all day yesterday to convince Hamish there had to be some other explanation for what they'd heard Taj saying. Okay, so he hadn't known Bodhi for very long, but still, his gut instinct was telling him (*screaming* at him) that Bodhi just wouldn't do something like that.

Hamish, on the other hand, had also been practically screaming at him that it was blindingly obvious Taj had been getting Bodhi to steal the goods and Taj had been selling them on to somebody else – the 'somebody' on

99

the other end of the phone. He stubbornly refused to listen when Angus argued Bodhi would never do anything like that.

"You're the one who says we have to follow the evidence," he'd said, "and this evidence says those two are somehow involved." And then the stinger, "Told you they were no good."

Reluctantly, Angus had agreed to try and video the meeting between Taj and the 'somebody' if only to try to prove it had nothing to do with the thefts. Of course, it had to be Angus that did the videoing as Hamish couldn't get away from the Helicopter for so much as five minutes and would right now be in the middle of a piano lesson or maths tutoring or something.

"Well, that's very convenient for you, isn't it?" Angus had muttered last night.

"Come on, Angus, crikey," Hamish had replied. "You know I'll be with you in spirit."

Angus was pretty sure that wasn't going to help. And he felt bad because he'd told Dad he was going to the park to see if Bodhi was there and he'd definitely be back by five for swimming training. It wasn't a lie because after he was finished with the recording he *would* see if Bodhi was in the park. But still, he knew Dad wouldn't be exactly happy if he knew what he was really up to.

Now he peered around the side of the bin to see if there was any sign of Taj yet. It was only a very small set of shops – a convenience store, bakery, Indian Restaurant, bottle shop and an empty shop where the video rental place had been before downloading straight from the internet had put it, and all other video rentals, out of business.

No sign of Taj. Angus watched a young mother push a pram into the convenience store, the baby bawling its head off. Out the front of the hairdresser's stood two older women having an animated conversation about something. They were laughing. Angus looked at his watch again. Right on four o'clock. Maybe the meeting had been called off?

No such luck. At that very moment, Angus spotted Taj up the road heading towards the shops on foot. He wasn't carrying anything (Hamish had been certain he'd have a big box of stolen goods to hand over), and as he entered the car park he walked right past Angus's hiding spot behind the industrial bin. His heart pounded loudly in his ears and his fingers were shaking as he opened the camera's view finder and pushed the 'record' button. The little red symbol blinked at him expectantly.

A black four-wheel drive pulled in behind Taj and parked across from the convenience store without stopping the engine. Taj walked up to it, opened the passenger side door and climbed in. Angus, recording the whole thing, could see there was a dark haired man driving while another man sat in the back. Taj and the driver talked for a while – Taj kept shaking his head while the driver seemed to be wagging his finger back at him.

Suddenly, the passenger side door opened and Taj jumped out and started walking away fast back toward Angus. The driver then opened *his* door, jumped out, rounded the vehicle and walked fast after Taj, calling his name. Taj wheeled around to face him. The second man got out of the back and joined them. The driver was thin, had a long nose, neat dark hair and what looked like a scar running from the left corner of his mouth almost to his left ear. He was dressed in a smart dark suit, which didn't go with his mean-looking face, which was screwed up in a grimace. The second man was shorter, but broad and muscular, his bulging, heavily-tattooed biceps clearly visible in his singlet. He was so muscled he didn't seem to be able to put his arms down flat against his sides but instead held them out like a gorilla. He was chewing gum with big, opened-mouth movements. An odd-looking couple.

Despite the group being reasonably close to Angus, he couldn't hear much of what they were saying because they were talking in fierce but hushed voices. Scarface said something about 'in the warehouse' and 'better change your attitude' while the Gorilla looked on, chewing his gum and smirking. Taj was obviously trying to put on a tough 'whatever' face but underneath Angus could see he was scared. Finally, he said something to the other two and turned and walked away again. This time they let him go. He strode fast by Angus and out of the car park. Scarface and The Gorilla continued to talk for a bit before moving back toward the four-wheel drive.

Now extremely uncomfortable from being in a cramped kneeling position for so long, Angus tried to change positions but lost his balance and tipped sideways into his bike which had been leaning against the back of the industrial bin also hidden from view. He and his bike tumbled backwards into a bunch of discarded soft drink bottles. The resulting clanging and clashing could probably have been heard on the moon. Oh God.

Holding the video-camera aloft, he scrambled to his feet amongst the bottles still rattling and rolling around.

"What the...? Hey! You kid!" bellowed a deep, rough voice. Scarface. Of course, they'd heard the noise and his hiding place was blown.

"He's got a camera! Get him!" Scarface and the Gorilla started towards Angus who wanted nothing more than to get on his bike and get out of there immediately. But his legs wouldn't work. And there was no one around. The laughing ladies were long gone. Should he yell for help and hope a shopkeeper would come out?

They were only a couple of metres away when his legs finally remembered how to move so he pushed the camera into his pocket, jumped on his bike and pedalled like never before, his heart beating so fast he wondered vaguely if he might have a heart attack. With a quick glance back over his shoulder, he saw Scarface and the Gorilla turn and rush back towards their vehicle, probably hoping to chase him down. But Angus had lived in the area his whole life and knew it inside out. With a sharp left, he was on the bike path which led up between the houses, too narrow for any car to follow, and away out of sight.

Chapter 17

The EKKA

"Happy birthday!" Angus handed his present to Hamish. Mrs McLeod, Ryan and his mum, Mrs Evans, all watched around the McLeod kitchen table as a grinning Hamish tore at the Avengers wrapping paper.

"Cool! Thanks!" Hamish held up the gifts. There was a book about Steve Irwin that came with a DVD of never-before-seen footage, plus a Lego Clone Troopers vs Droidekas.

"I can help you with it," said Angus. "If you want." He was hoping to make up for the Starfighter he'd started with Bodhi.

Last night, he and Hamish had reviewed the video-footage and discussed at length Angus's lucky escape the day before. Although he was reluctant, Angus thought it was probably time to tell their parents. He'd had a huge fright yesterday and what if Scarface and the Gorilla spotted him at the park or the shops? He didn't like the idea of being afraid for the rest of his life.

"Just wait until after the Ekka," Hamish had begged. "Otherwise the Helicopter will totally freak out and likely cancel the whole trip." So that settled it. Sunday they would tell.

Now the two mothers were discussing the school thefts.

"...and poor Patricia Nesbit is so upset about the iPad she'd bought for her granddaughter, honestly, it's just dreadful," said Mrs Evans.

"Who'd want a stupid *Dora-the-Explorer* iPad anyway?" muttered Ryan.

"Oh, was it Dora? How cute. Well, that just makes it even worse," said his mother.

"All right, that's enough unpleasantness, come on, wee-uns!" said Mrs McLeod in her thick Scottish accent. "It's time to go have some fun at the Ekka!" And with that, she bustled everyone out the door and the three boys into the car.

"Bye, have fun and be good, Ryan," said Mrs Evans, waving.

"Buckle up, boys," said Mrs McLeod, starting the car. "Now, we will buy lunch at the Ekka but I've been canny enough to also pack some snacks. Angus, darlin', have a wee brownie, baked fresh this mornin'," she said, passing back a Tupperware container.

The Ekka was a wonderland of sights and smells. Angus looked around wide-eyed, the way he always did here, trying to drink in everything at once. After entering through Gate 4 they passed by the cattle and horse pavilions with the unmistakable waft of animals, poo and sawdust which mixed in a strangely pleasant way with the smell of hot chips, smoky wood-fired pizzas and waffle cones. A voice blared incoherently from the loudspeakers over the top of manic carnival music.

Passing by the enormous show ring, they stopped to watch a few quick-fire rounds of the woodchopping. Man, those guys were amazing. They could chop wood while standing on tiny platforms metres in the air. Then on they went toward the famous show bag pavilion, being careful to stay together as a group.

"Mind you stay close, boys!" sang Mrs McLeod approximately every thirty seconds, "we don't want anyone getting lost!" Of course, Mrs McLeod had given the boys each a wrist band to wear which had her name and mobile number on it, "just in case".

There *were* people everywhere. Young, old, and in between were all chattering and laughing non-stop and walking and running every which way. All around kids clutched ice-creams or balloons, *or both*. Angus looked on as one little girl had a complete meltdown, screaming her head off because she'd dropped her ice-cream in the dirt *and* let her balloon go at the same time. It was a helium-filled Barbie balloon and he watched it sail high into the air and drift away towards the Ferris wheel.

The crowd was thick outside the show bag pavilion as people came and went with their treasures. Angus got a fright for a second when he saw a man who looked a lot like Scarface. It couldn't be, could it? At the Ekka? The man disappeared quickly into the throng before he could be certain and Angus shook his head. You're being stupid, he said to himself, just still a bit shaky from yesterday and seeing things that aren't there.

Luckily for them the queue at the show bag pavilion didn't stretch too far. Angus had never seen so many show bags in his life and he stared in wonder at the overwhelming choice displayed on the surrounding walls. Show bag heaven. But all three boys knew exactly what they wanted and before long Angus, Hamish and Ryan each had the much sought-after Avengers bag dangling from their arms. Angus's mum had given him some extra money to get Liam a Karate Ninja Deluxe Bag and he managed to do that also.

"Oh, go on, why don't you each have a wee Bertie Beetle show bag, too?" said Mrs McLeod as she handed over more money to the bored-looking teenager behind the counter. The Bertie Beetle chocolate bags were great value at only two dollars each.

"But don't eat all the chocolate at once or you'll be sick!"

With show bags secured and a couple of Bertie Beetles scoffed it was time for some serious ride action in side-show alley. They had two goes on the dodgems, the second one ending early after Hamish hilariously caused a major pile-up, the cars getting so jammed together the ride had to be halted while a maintenance guy was called in to fix things. They lined up for rides with names like the Cha-Cha, the Sizzler, and the Boom Boom, each one involving having their bodies strapped in before being hurled about with tremendous force, backwards, forwards, sideways, and every other which-ways. It was epic.

But then there was the Freak Out, an 'extreme' ride. The Freak Out looked like a giant kitchen stick blender. Ride-goers were strapped onto the end of it and spun around upside down perilously high in the air. Angus knew what his limits were and decided he was already plenty freaked-out enough, thank you very much. Ryan agreed with him and neither of them would budge as Hamish begged them to go on the ride with him. In the end, he probably would have gone on it alone except his mother stepped in and said no way.

It was a good thing Mrs McLeod, who wasn't born yesterday as she was fond of saying, had led them to the rides *before* lunch and not after. Lunch consisted of plump, golden dagwood dogs dripping with tomato sauce, chocolate milkshakes and, for dessert, the Ekka's famous strawberry sundaes. Not even Hamish felt much like spinning around upside down after all that.

The plan for the afternoon was to get a good seat at the show ring and watch the sheep dog trials and try to wait patiently for the monster truck spectacular. It would be an awesome way to finish the day. On the way to the show ring, they all stopped to watch a guy on stilts perform his juggling act.

Later, Angus would think about how that was the moment it all went wrong.

He needed to go to the toilet. Looking around, he saw a toilet block right behind them and asked Mrs McLeod if he could just duck in. She insisted Hamish go too (it was one of her Ekka rules that nobody went anywhere alone) and took their show bags. As they went to enter the toilet block, who should they run into but Finn from school! Hamish stopped to chat with Finn for a minute and to check out his show bags, but Angus was busting.

"Hi," he said and darted in to the toilet.

Washing his hands at the basin, he was thinking about monster trucks when his skin suddenly felt prickly. It was as if the air pressure had changed or something. Something was...wrong. Uneasily, he looked up into the mirror. Standing over him, smirking hideously back in the mirror, was Scarface!

"Well, well, if it isn't camera boy," he said with an amused sneer.

Okay, have to get out fast. Angus tried to dash past, half-ducking as he went, but Scarface grabbed hold of his jacket collar.

"What's the rush, mate? You and I have some catching up to do. I want that camera. And you're going to give it to me."

Where the heck was Hamish?

"Come with me," said Scarface and began to pull at him. Angus was about to start screaming as loudly as he could when a father with two little boys came barrelling in. Distracted, Scarface loosened his grip enough that Angus wrenched free and made a lunge for the door. The toilet block had two entrances and he was forced to head for the far one in order to get past Scarface. That meant he exited on the other side, away from where Mrs McLeod and the others were waiting.

With his heart once again in his throat, Angus tore off. A quick look over his shoulder told him Scarface was hot on his heels. Dodging people and prams, Angus had the advantage of being small and nimble, and a good runner. Sidestepping an elderly lady, he dashed into the crowded Fresh Food Pavilion. Past the apples and oranges, past the pineapple and banana display, he hoped the crowd would help him lose the terrifying Scarface. And it might have, too, except he stood on some dropped grapes, skidded and nearly lost his balance before righting himself. With Scarface gaining on him, Angus fled out the nearest exit, raced around the Dairy Hall, up some steps and found himself in Animal Boulevard.

Halfway down the centre aisle, past the goats, calves, and ducks, he risked a look back to see Scarface hurtle through the door and stop and scan the crowd. Searching for him, obviously, and made more difficult by a large school group, bless them, in the middle of the pavilion. Thinking quickly Angus knelt down and squeezed between the railings of the closest pen. He crouched in the corner, using the railings for cover. Half a dozen very surprised piglets looked at him in astonishment but unless Scarface actually peered over the railings he wouldn't see him.

The seconds ticked by. He risked a peek through the railings. Scarface had come up the aisle and was just metres away, eyes darting furiously. Angus made himself as small as he could. A mobile phone rang. Scarface was right beside him on the other side of the railing. He could see the man's shiny, polished black shoes between the gap of the lower railings. Scarface muttered a swear word and then the phone stopped ringing.

"What?... No...I'm at the Ekka. You won't believe it but I'm in the animal thing, chasing that kid. The kid who had the camera!...Yeah." Then, more impatiently, "No, the bantam hens won't get judged until three o'clock...For my mother, you idiot!...yeah, win every year."

Angus couldn't hear what else was said as Scarface walked away. So he was here to show his mother's prize winning bantam hens. If things weren't so serious, Angus might have laughed out loud. As it was, he saw something on the ground right where Scarface had been standing. It looked like a small card of some kind. He sneaked his hand out and picked it up. Scarface must have dropped it when he took out his phone, Angus was certain it hadn't been there before. Dropping the card straight into his jacket pocket without looking at it, his intention now was to sit tight until Scarface left the pavilion. Peeking over the top railing, Angus watched his back retreat down the aisle until he was almost at the door. And it all would have been fine except right at that moment one of the animal attendants spotted him in the pig stall and called out.

"Hey, you! You're not allowed in there!"

Scarface turned and saw Angus who jumped over the railing and tore off again toward the far exit, dodging toddlers and grannies. Once again, Scarface was hot in pursuit. Angus jumped the exit steps and was now outside. He sprinted up the side of the Animal Pavilion, past Expo place and glanced back to see Scarface still after him.

He turned and, panicking a little, headed straight through the nearest door which was another toilet block so he should have been able to run straight out the exit on the other side. Oh no, this toilet block didn't *have* another exit! He was trapped! Certain Scarface had seen him go in, Angus did the only thing he could do which was to run into the only empty toilet stall available and lock the door. In complete panic now, he looked under the door to see Scarface's shiny black shoes enter the toilet block. How was he going to get out of this? He couldn't sit in this toilet stall all day.

Looking around, Angus realised he was in the end stall, meaning it butted up against the outer cement wall. High up on the wall was a small window. An open window. Without waiting to think too much about it, he climbed up on top of the toilet cistern, reached across, grabbed the window ledge with both hands and swung himself up.

"Hey!" yelled Scarface who could see him now above the toilet door. But Angus didn't wait around. In a second, he had himself through the window and leapt down to the ground, being careful to land on bended knees. Knowing Scarface would certainly be running around the toilet block to catch him, he turned and took off. He rounded a corner and – CRASH! He'd smacked straight into a man. A large bald man with a badge and a walkie-talkie. A SECURITY OFFICER!!

"Whoa there, sonny! Where's the fire?" said the security guy with his hands on Angus's shoulders. He looked around to see Scarface standing back about ten metres, panting heavily.

"Um...I'm lost," said Angus, turning back to the security guard and trying his best to sound upset, which wasn't hard because he was, in fact, *very* upset. "I can't find my friends. Can you please help me?" At this, Scarface slipped silently away into the crowd.

The Security Officer took Angus back to Mrs McLeod and the others, still standing by the toilets. Finn was still there with his mum and dad. Mrs McLeod was busy talking to another security officer when they walked up.

"What will I tell his mother? This is the most dreadful thing!" And then she saw Angus.

"Oh, Angus! There you are! Thank goodness! Where have you been! We thought you were lost. I was about to have a heart attack!" She grabbed him and hugged him close until he couldn't breathe.

When he was finally able to prise himself free enough to talk, he explained how he'd gotten confused, gone out the wrong exit of the toilet and, yes, had become a bit lost. Sorry about that.

"Crikey!" said Hamish.

"Were you scared?" asked Ryan.

"Epic fail," laughed Finn.

For the rest of the day, he stuck close to Mrs McLeod (who wasn't going to let him out of her sight anyway). Although he kept a look out, he didn't see Scarface again. He watched the monster truck show mostly in silence, eating the muffins and brownies handed to him by Mrs McLeod. The show was good; lots of enormous trucks with monster faces rampaging around and crushing small cars into oblivion. Even so, Angus felt he could have done without extra excitement.

Chapter 18

In Trouble Again

"Heaps under here, help me roll it over," said Hamish.

Angus knelt down on the grass beside him and together they pushed the half-rotted log over. Dozens of cockroaches scurried about on the damp earth trying to escape the Sunday morning sunlight in Angus's backyard. The two of them scraped up the cockies, dropping them into the jar. Dinner for the waterdragons.

"You know, the Helicopter was spinning out of control when you disappeared yesterday," said Hamish as he screwed on the lid. "I was sure she was going to crash," he said, chuckling, "she was so angry with me for not going into the toilet with you."

Angus had told him all about the chase by Scarface. "I still can't believe he was there. And for a chook competition!"

"Bantam hens," said Angus. "And you can believe it. He was there and he almost got me."

"Well, they're seriously bad dudes. Him and the Gorilla. And your mate Bodhi and her brother are mixed up with them. Are we going to tell your dad today?"

Angus frowned. He still couldn't believe Bodhi had anything to do with them.

"Far out, Angus, don't forget she's standing back and letting you take the blame. Some friend."

"We still don't really have any evidence of anything," said Angus. "Maybe Scarface was just angry because he doesn't like being videoed by a stranger."

"You've got to be kidding me," said Hamish.

Angus reached into his jacket pocket to get a tissue to wipe the dirt from his fingers when he felt something. He pulled out a card.

"I totally forgot about this," he said, looking at it. "Scarface dropped it yesterday." He and Hamish read what was written on the card.

"Warehouse. 147 Enterprise Avenue."

"Oh!" Hamish was suddenly excited. "Remember in the video-footage of the meeting with Taj, Scarface said something about a warehouse? This must be it!"

Angus shrugged his shoulders. He didn't like where this was going.

"Don't you get it?" Hamish was practically hopping up and down. "This will be where they keep the stolen

119

goods until they sell them on or whatever they do. You said we didn't have any evidence. This is where the evidence is! Let's go check it out!"

"Are you crazy? What if they're there?"

"Won't be anyone there on a Sunday," said Hamish, putting the jar of cockroaches in his pocket.

"Well, how are *we* going to check it out? You know the Helicopter doesn't let you ride around the streets unsupervised and don't even *think* about asking me to go by myself," said Angus.

"She won't know," Hamish said, smiling. "She thinks I'm spending the morning at your place. She won't be picking me up until after lunch."

Angus considered this.

"You don't have your bike."

"I'll ride Liam's," said Hamish.

Angus supposed it couldn't hurt to just go and have a look. Okay, it probably could hurt but he decided to do it anyway.

First, they had to go and find the street on Whereis.com. Fortunately, his week of being banned from his iPad was over. He couldn't help hoping the street would be somewhere on the other side of Brisbane, or the world even, just somewhere way too far away for them to ride to. As it turned out, however, it was in an industrial estate on the edge of their suburb. An easy ten minute ride away.

"Let's go," said Hamish. Then he added, "Don't worry, Angus, I'll have your back this time."

Angus wasn't sure that made him feel any better, but he told Dad they were going for a bike ride and wouldn't be too long.

He felt uncomfortable as they pedalled along in silence, the sun warm on their faces. Mrs McLeod would freak if she knew Hamish was riding around the streets and he, Angus, was already in enough trouble with Mum and Dad and here he was headed for a warehouse where he might run into some scary dudes, one of whom had chased him and nearly caught him only yesterday. What was he thinking?

He was thinking of Bodhi. Going to this warehouse might somehow prove she wasn't involved, although he didn't know how.

Eventually they arrived at Enterprise Avenue. They stopped at the corner and stared up the street. Everything was quiet. Being Sunday, the place was bare of cars and people. Distant traffic could be heard zooming along the motorway to the south. It was eerie. The street was lined with large warehouses with signs advertising things like Mike's Plumbing Supplies, A-Plus Forklift Hire, The Hungry Pig Catering Corner.

Angus looked over at Hamish, who seemed less sure of the whole thing now. Still, they'd come this far.

"Come on," said Angus.

Slowly, they started riding again, looking out for the right number warehouse.

"When we get to it," said Angus, "we'll see if we can have a quick peek in a window or something and then go, right?"

"Right. Look, there it is. Number 147," said Hamish.

A big nondescript-looking warehouse stared back at them from the right hand side of the street. It was the same as all the others except it had no signs out the front advertising a business of any sort. There were no cars parked in the few car parking bays, although there was also a driveway leading around the back. A large red roller door fronted the building with a small regular-sized people door on its right. There were no windows at the front but from their approach the boys could see a small window down the right hand side of the building.

"Okay, let's do it and get out of here," said Hamish.

Leaving their bikes and helmets just inside the driveway, they went around the side to see if they could see in the window. It was too high.

Angus looked around. "Look, there's an old milk crate over against the fence," he said. "If we stand on it, we should be able to see in."

They brought the milk crate over. There was only room for one of them to climb up so Angus stepped up and peered in the window.

What was this? He stared in confusion and then astonishment as he realised what he was looking at. He couldn't see any stolen iPads. What he saw were half a dozen vehicles, cars and utes, in the process of being spray-painted. Didn't Dad say just the other day that John, a neighbour in their street, had had his ute stolen? And a car from the school, too? One of the utes looked familiar. He was looking through the window straight at John's stolen ute! He knew it was John's because he could clearly see his personalised number plate "Jono5". It used to be black but it was now in the process of being painted blue.

"Oh God," said Angus.

"What? What's in there?" said Hamish impatiently.

"Stolen cars! They're not stealing iPads, they're stealing cars! We need to get out of here, quick!"

But it was too late. Angus had been so focussed on what he could see in the window and Hamish so busy peering up at Angus that neither of them had heard footsteps approaching.

"I don't think so, brats," said a voice.

The Gorilla.

Right behind them.

Before they could run, the Gorilla had them both in a tight grip. Angus struggled, but it was no use. Hamish looked as panicked as Angus felt.

"Now you're here you may as well stay and visit," the Gorilla said with a raspy laugh.

"Let us go! Help!" shouted Angus as loudly as he could. But the Gorilla only kept laughing at him.

"Yell as loud as you want. There's no one to hear you." And with that he dragged both boys to the door and pushed them through it.

Chapter 19

Captives

Inside, the warehouse stank of paint, petrol and oil fumes. Still being held tightly by the Gorilla, Angus could see now that all the vehicles were either in the process of being spray-painted or up on blocks being stripped of parts. The Gorilla slammed the door shut with his foot.

"Hey, Boss!" he called. "Come and see what the cat dragged in."

On one side of the warehouse, there was a door with a sign reading "Office". The door opened and out strode Scarface. He stopped in his tracks when he saw Angus and Hamish. A thin-lipped smile began to slowly form on his face, making his scar stretch weirdly. It was the most chilling smile Angus had ever seen.

"Caught them looking in the window," said Gorilla.

"Well, well," said Scarface, walking over to them slowly. "If it isn't camera boy and a little friend. And here I was still upset about you getting away yesterday and now today you come walking straight into my arms. How wonderful. Did you enjoy the Ekka?"

"You have to let us go!" said Angus, trying to sound firm and brave when he'd never been more frightened in his life.

Hamish was as white as a ghost and starting to wheeze. His asthma always played up when he was upset.

"No, I don't," said Scarface. "What I wanted was to get that camera off you. But now that you've stumbled upon our little operation here..." He let that hang in the air.

"We can't let them go now, Boss," said Gorilla. "I heard them. This one's worked it all out," he said, giving Angus a little shake. "They'll go straight to the cops if we let them go."

"No, we won't," tried Angus, desperately. "We won't tell anyone. We promise."

"Hmmm...what to do, what to do?" said Scarface, looking down and tapping his lips with a finger. He looked up again.

"My associate and I have to go out for about half an hour. That will give me some thinking time to work out what to do with you. In the meantime, let's put you somewhere safe."

They were half-dragged, half-pushed into the office by the Gorilla as Hamish pulled his asthma inhaler out of his pocket. But he fumbled and dropped it and the Gorilla kicked it away. It went skidding across the floor.

"He needs that! He's asthmatic!" Angus tried.

Both men ignored him. As they were pulled across the room, Angus took in a desk and filing cabinet against one wall and an old wooden cupboard, kind of a wardrobe with a sliding door in the corner, which it seemed they were headed for.

"In you go," said Scarface, opening the cupboard door. It was empty.

The Gorilla pushed them both inside and slid the door shut. Angus heard a padlock click shut and then footsteps heading away. Hamish was wheezing.

"Hey! He needs his inhaler!" Angus shouted. "Please!"

A door slammed and he heard a car that must have been parked around the back start up. It drove along the side of the warehouse and then away up the street.

The cupboard was dark and musty. And scary.

"What are we...gonna do?" Hamish panted, his wheezing even worse now. "We've got to... get out. Can't breathe."

"Okay, try to stay calm," said Angus, trying hard to stay calm himself. "I'll think of something."

This was bad. Hamish was struggling for air and Angus knew he was panicked. It was going to be up to him to get them out. Scarface had said they'd be gone for about half an hour. But Hamish didn't have half an hour.

Dear God, what was he going to do?

Chapter 20

In the Cupboard

Angus had to stay calm. If he panicked now it was all over for Hamish.

"Sit on the floor," he told him and Hamish did, not that there was much room.

Angus heaved hard against the bolted door. It didn't budge. He hadn't thought it would but it was worth a try. Now he began to use his hands to feel slowly around the inside of the cupboard, touching all along the walls top to bottom. Thin fibro. Good.

He ran his hands along the bottom of the narrow left hand side of the cupboard. What was this? It was all rough and bumpy down here whereas the rest of the wall was smooth to touch. Water damage? If so, it meant there was a chance the fibro had deteriorated in this spot. With any luck it had rotted away a bit.

"I'm going to try and kick this wall out here. I think it's been water-damaged. Move back as far as you can."

Hamish didn't answer but shuffled back a bit, rasping and wheezing badly.

"Okay, I'm going to kick on the count of three. One. Two. Three!" and Angus unleashed the biggest kick he could manage in the cramped space, trying to aim his heel directly at the water-damaged part of the wall. There was a cracking a sound.

"Yes!" he said in excitement and he felt the wall with his hand. There was a crack. It *was* half rotted away.

"Look out, I'm going to have another go."

Smack!

Smack!

On the third kick, there was a crunching and tearing as the bottom part of the cupboard side gave way. A jagged hole about thirty centimetres square at the bottom appeared, letting in light and much-needed air.

"It's okay, Hamish, we're going to get out."

Again, Hamish didn't answer and Angus knew he was in bad shape. On the spot he decided to try and wriggle through the hole and find the inhaler quickly. This was difficult as there was barely enough room to get down on the floor in order to try and squeeze out. Grunting and squirming, he thought he'd gotten himself stuck but then a bit more of the wall came away as he wiggled his hips. And finally he was out.

Clambering up, he looked around wildly. There! The inhaler had been kicked under the desk. He scrambled over, grabbed it and raced back to the cupboard. As the door was padlocked Hamish was going to have to squeeze out the hole Angus had made but first he needed to breathe.

"Hamish! I've got your inhaler, here!" He bent down and thrust his arm in through the hole. At first nothing happened. Why didn't Hamish grab it? Oh God, was he too late?

But then he felt Hamish's clammy hand take the inhaler. For a whole minute, Hamish stayed inside the cupboard taking deep breaths of his medication. Finally, his blond head appeared at the hole. He grinned up at Angus but his face was deathly pale and his hair drenched in sweat.

"Thanks," he said.

Angus helped pull him out and onto his feet. As he did so he bumped against something hard in Hamish's pocket.

"What's that?"

"I dunno. Oh, the cockroaches," said Hamish pulling the jar free.

"Give it to me." Hamish handed it over and Angus put it into his own pocket.

They looked at one another. Now what? Although they were out of the cupboard and Hamish was breathing normally again, they were still trapped in the warehouse.

"Come on," he said at last, "let's get out before they come back!" The office door stood open but when they ran to the door leading to the outside they found it deadlocked. It would take a key to open it. But Angus wasn't beaten yet.

"Let's see if we can find a key in the office. Or a phone so we can call the police."

They ran back into the office. There was no phone, so they searched frantically for a key. Angus looked in the filing cabinet while Hamish checked the desk drawers.

"So these guys have nothing to do with the school thefts?" said Hamish, opening a drawer.

"Doesn't look like it. Only the car that was stolen. These are big-time crooks, I think," said Angus.

"Great," said Hamish. "Ugh! A mouldy pizza," and he slammed the drawer shut. "These guys are pigs."

When at last it became obvious there was no key to be found, they ran back out the front and tried pulling on the big, heavy chain that manually operated the huge roller door. Nothing. It wouldn't budge. They weren't strong enough. Angus began to feel sick with defeat. There was no way out.

Hang on, the window! The one he'd looked in at from the outside.

"We're so stupid," he said to Hamish. "We can get out the window, look." He pointed up at it frantically.

"But it's too high," said Hamish.

"I'll climb up on the chair from the office, smash it with something and we'll be able to climb out. Come on, help me get the chair."

But before they could move they heard a key twisting in the door. Scarface and the Gorilla were back.

Chapter 21

A Team Effort

As the key turned in the lock, Angus felt furious with himself. He should have thought of the window straight away. Now it was too late. The door to the warehouse flew open and Scarface and Gorilla sauntered in.

"What the..." said the Gorilla, stopping in surprise when he saw them.

"Hmm, so you got out of the cupboard. Clever," said Scarface, right behind him.

Angus slowly put his hand into his jacket pocket.

"You have to let us go," he said. "My parents know where we are." As he spoke he was trying to secretly get the lid off the jar of cockroaches.

"Nice try, but I don't think they know anything," said Scarface, his scar twitching, all red and angry-looking.

"Enough chat. We're going for a little ride, boys," and he pointed behind Angus and Hamish to a blue late model Holden sedan that had its boot open.

"Hop in," he said.

"Wh-what?" stammered Hamish, looking back and forth between the boot, Angus and Scarface. "You can't make us get in the b-boot."

Angus's fingers were still working furiously inside his pocket to loosen the lid of the jar. It was a tricky task with only one hand.

"Sure we can," said the Gorilla and he and Scarface started to come towards them. At that moment, the lid came off the jar and Angus pulled it from his pocket. He hurled the mass of wriggling, squirming cockroaches right into the Gorilla's stunned face. Several ran inside his gaping mouth.

"Arghh!" he shrieked, spitting cockroaches, and batting hard at his face with both hands. "Get them off, get them off!"

Angus hurled the empty jar at Scarface's surprised head. It missed, shattering on the ground instead.

"Quick, run!" Angus shouted at Hamish, but Scarface was between them and the door. Could the two of them take him down?

All of a sudden there was movement behind the men. Someone was rushing in through the open door. It was Bodhi!

She charged at Scarface, leapt into the air and with a flying kick to his back sent him sprawling. He landed hard on his face with her still on top of him.

"COME ON!" Angus shouted at Hamish and Bodhi.

Hamish ran for the door but Bodhi was struggling to scramble off Scarface as he made wild grabs at this girl on his back who'd come from nowhere. Hamish turned at the door, screaming at them to hurry up.

Angus grabbed Bodhi's arm and half-pulling, half-dragging her, they somehow made it to Hamish. Together they fell through the door into the bright sunlight with Scarface right behind them, snarling and swearing.

As they were about to run for their lives, a car came screaming into the driveway nearly running them over. It was Taj in the Ford. And behind him were two police cars, lights flashing.

The three of them ran to Taj as police poured from their cars and bolted into the warehouse, shouting "STOP! POLICE! HANDS IN THE AIR!"

Chapter 22

Motive and Opportunity

At the police station, the story of what happened unfolded. Everyone's parents were present (Mrs McLeod looking as though she might suffer a heart attack at any moment) as each person told their part of the tale. After Angus and Hamish finished talking, Bodhi calmly told how she'd spotted the boys on their bikes from her veranda high up on the hill. She said she knew that Hamish didn't like her much (Hamish had the good grace to look embarrassed at this) but wasn't particularly bothered because some people like you and some don't and that's life. Besides, she was bored silly and desperate for something to do so she jumped on her own bike to join them, assuming they were going to the park. But when the boys rode straight past the park, she decided to hang back and follow from a distance, curious about where they were going. As Angus and Hamish were dragged into the warehouse by the Gorilla, Bodhi was up the street watching, shocked and horrified. She raced

137

home as fast as she could to get help from Taj, but he wasn't at home and wasn't answering his phone. She left a frantic voice mail message for him and then rode her bike straight back to the warehouse to try and do whatever she could to help the boys.

Picking up the story, Taj explained how as soon as he'd heard Bodhi's message he called the police and told them where to go, then jumped in the car to meet them there.

Scarface and the Gorilla were indeed running a car stealing operation from the warehouse. Taj had known them a couple of years ago. They'd heard he was back in town and were trying to force him into stealing cars for them again. The phone conversation Angus and Hamish had overheard had been Taj telling them he wouldn't steal cars for them, he was starting a new life now and they'd better stay away from his sister's school.

Later, as they left the police station, Hamish was looking at Bodhi with new respect.

"What are you, anyway? Some kind of Ninja?" he said without a hint of sarcasm as they went down the steps.

She smiled. "I know some karate."

"Black belt," said Taj, opening the car door for her. "Watch her, she's lethal."

Although everything had turned out okay, Mrs McLeod told Hamish he wouldn't be leaving the house again until he was thirty. Hamish said that was fine with him. When Angus got home, he went straight to his iPad and handed it to his mother.

"I'm guessing you'll be keeping this for at least a month," he said. "If you need me, I'll be pulling weeds out the back." Liam chased after him demanding details, super-excited that his bike had played a part in a daring adventure.

Later, unexpectedly, his mother returned his iPad. He hadn't actually broken any rules, she said. In fact, he'd stayed level-headed and acted with courage to save his friend by getting them out of the cupboard. She was proud of him.

The next day, the boys at school couldn't believe what they were hearing as Angus and Hamish retold the story.

"Awesome," said Luke. "I'm gonna start karate lessons."

"That'd be dangerous," said Finn, rolling his eyes.

"Amazing story," said Ryan.

"Yes, that is without a doubt the most commoving tale I've ever heard," said Perry, chewing an apple.

"Did you just say 'commoving'?" asked Finn, looking at Perry with arched eyebrows. "What the heck does 'commoving' mean?"

"It's a synonym for exciting," said Perry and he casually took another bite of his apple.

Finn rolled his eyes again.

"Do you know any synonyms for 'annoying' or 'ridiculous'?"

"Is that a rhetorical question?" shot back Perry.

Ignoring him, Finn turned back to Angus and Hamish.

"Okay, cool story indeed, and you guys may have uncovered a major car theft operation and everything, but you never did actually figure out who was taking the phones and stuff from the school, did you?"

"No," admitted Angus. It had been weighing heavily on him. As far as the rest of the school was concerned, he was still a thief and he'd uncovered not one shred of evidence as to the identity of the real culprit.

"It's an epic fail on that one," he admitted.

"Bodhi!" called out Hamish suddenly. All the boys looked up to see Bodhi walking alone on the path. "Wanna play handball?"

That afternoon, after homework was done, Angus lay on his bed and watched his model solar system rotate. He was thinking once again of his complete failure to clear his own name. It looked as if Hamish would indeed be going to the National Robotics championships in Sydney without him.

Around and around went the planets. He thought again about motive and opportunity. And what had Mr Jackson said? Something about looking closer to home. At the back of his mind something was nagging at him but he couldn't quite grasp what it was. It was like when you had a word on the tip of your tongue but couldn't quite get it out.

Liam burst into the room.

"Look what I got Clancy for her birthday!" he sang, plonking himself down on the bed beside Angus. He was holding up a Dora the Explorer backpack. Liam was going to his classmate's party on the weekend.

"Hmm. That's nice," said Angus distractedly.

Dora the Explorer.

Close to home.

Motive.

Opportunity.

"Ahhhh!" Angus sat bolt upright, nearly knocking Liam off the bed. "Holy cow!" he said. "I KNOW WHO IT IS!"

Chapter 23

The Thief

After school the next day, Mrs Evans, Ryan's mum, held a special afternoon tea. Angus and his mother were there on Ryan's back patio, as was Hamish and his mother, despite the fact that Hamish was not yet thirty.

The Evans family had received some wonderful news. New tests had shown Ryan's dad was recovering and he should be back at work in only a few weeks. They wouldn't need to seek treatment in America, after all.

Mrs Evans looked more relaxed and happy than she had in a long time as she sliced a chocolate mud cake and passed around huge chunks. Ryan tried to fit an entire piece into his mouth at once and nearly choked laughing when it couldn't be done. Angus thought he also looked as though the weight of the world had been lifted from his shoulders.

This made Angus feel even worse about what he had to do.

After the boys had eaten as much watermelon, chocolate cake and mini cheesecakes as they could manage (the mini cheesecakes baked and brought by Mrs McLeod), Ryan asked his mother if they could go play in his room.

"Okay, love," she said. "Just try be a bit quiet while your father's resting."

Ryan and Hamish sat on the bed and pored over Ryan's new, special, limited edition Avengers comic book, commenting on this and that while Angus watched them silently from a chair.

"You okay?" asked Hamish, eventually looking up at him.

"Yeah," he said. "I'm just still thinking about how someone stole all those things from the school. And how we still don't know who it is."

"I know," said Hamish. "I wish you were coming to Sydney with me."

Angus looked at Ryan. "What do you think, Ryan?"

Ryan jerked his head up out of the comic. "What?" he said, glancing between Angus and Hamish.

"Do you have any idea who the thief is?" said Angus.

"Wh-why would I know?" stammered Ryan, looking a little flustered.

Hamish and Ryan were both looking at Angus. Once again, he was going to have to search deep for courage. He spoke quietly.

"It's you, Ryan. Isn't it? You've been stealing the things from school."

The comic book slipped from Ryan's hands and onto the floor with a thud.

Hamish, with his mouth open in astonishment looked back and forth between them. "Crikey," he said finally.

Ryan blinked and looked for a minute like he might run from the room. But then with a big heave his shoulders sank and he hung his head.

"Yes," he whispered.

"What!" said Hamish.

"Yes! Yes, it was me, okay?" He gave a violent sob. "I'm sorry, Angus. I didn't mean for you to get into trouble. I nearly got caught with Layla's phone and I dropped it into the nearest tray I could. It happened to be yours." He was crying hard now. "Please don't hate me."

He reached under the bed and pulled out a box. In the box were all the stolen iPads and laptops, including Mrs Nesbit's Dora the Explorer.

Hamish could not have looked more surprised if the comic book had jumped up off the floor and put itself back on the shelf.

Angus was calm. "But why, Ryan? Why did you want all this stuff?" he asked.

"Because Dad was sick and Mum didn't have enough money to buy the good medicine," he said, tears and snot streaming down his face. "I thought maybe I could sell it. But once I had it all, I didn't know what to do with it. I don't know any bad guys who buy stolen stuff. I realised it was a stupid idea but it was too late then. I didn't know what to do. That's why I've been feeling sick all the time, I felt so guilty and worried about being caught, as well as worried about the trouble I'd gotten you into.

I was going to try and give it all back but I accidently dropped Mrs Nesbit's mini-iPad and it broke and I didn't have any money to buy her another one." He pulled it out of the box and opened the cover. The screen was smashed.

Angus handed him a clean tissue from his pocket. Ryan put down the iPad, blew his nose loudly and then said, "You're not going to tell, are you? Please don't tell!"

"I'm not going to tell, Ryan," said Angus. "But you are. You have to."

Ryan looked up with red, swollen eyes.

"Ask your mother to come in here right now and explain everything to her. It'll be okay. Everything apart from the mini-iPad can be returned."

Hamish put his arm around Ryan and, finding his tongue at last, said, "Yeah, do it, mate. It's the brave thing to do. We'll help you."

Ryan looked at them both, sniffed, then called out for his mother.

Dora the Explorer was the key, Angus explained later to Hamish.

"Mrs Nesbit told me her stolen iPad had a Dora cover but I don't think it was general knowledge. I certainly didn't tell anyone. I meant to tell you but then I forgot all about it. And then before we left for the Ekka, Ryan said something about it. He *knew* it was a Dora the Explorer cover."

"Okay," said Hamish, "but his mum works at the school, so she could have known about it and told him."

"No, she didn't know, because when he mentioned it she was surprised to find out about it. Remember?" said Angus. "Anyway, I realised Ryan also had opportunity – he's often in classrooms after school helping his mum pack up and so could easily put stuff in his bag without her noticing. He also had motive. Everyone knew Ryan's family were doing it tough for money because his dad was sick and couldn't work. Anyway, when I put two and two together, I just felt sure I was right."

Ryan's parents returned everything to the school and promised to buy Mrs Nesbit a new iPad as soon as Mr Evans was working again. In the end, they didn't have to because Angus asked Mr Jackson if he'd help them raise money by holding a school car wash. Angus, Hamish and Ryan soaped and scrubbed enough cars to buy a new iPad-mini with a Dora the Explorer cover *and* a matching backpack. Mrs Nesbit and her granddaughter were thrilled.

Ryan received a stern talking-to from Mr Dingwall but wasn't suspended due to 'the mitigating circumstances' of his father having been so ill. 'Mitigating' had Perry scrambling for his notebook.

Once again, Angus found himself in the Principal's office, facing Mr Dingwall across the desk.

"I hope you'll accept my sincere apologies, Angus. A very unfortunate business all round." Mr Dingwall held out his hand.

Angus looked at it. As before, the clock ticked. But not as smugly.

"Thanks, Mr Dingwall." He shook the Principal's hand.

"Now, you better get along home and start packing for Sydney, young man."

YIPPEE!!

Have you read book 2?

Angus Adams and the Missing
Pro-Surfer
(The Free-Range Kid Mysteries Book 2)

Want to know when new Angus books come out?
Join Lee Winter's mailing list at **leeMwinter.com** and
we'll let you know ☺

You can email Lee at lee@leemwinter.com

Acknowledgments

Thank you to Mariela Reiss (www.asapediting.com) for her fantastic editing and positive energy.

Made in the USA
San Bernardino, CA
06 December 2018